P9-DJA-844

Geronimo Stilton

THE ENCHANTED CHARMS

THE SEVENTH ADVENTURE IN THE KINGDOM OF FANTASY

Scholastic Inc.

No part of this publication may be reproduced, stored in a retrieval system, or transmitted in any form or by any means, electronic, mechanical, photocopying, recording, or otherwise, without written permission from the copyright holder. For information regarding permission, please contact: Atlantyca S.p.A., Via Leopardi 8, 20123 Milan, Italy; e-mail foreignrights@atlantyca.it, www.atlantyca.com.

Library of Congress Cataloging-in-Publication Data Available

ISBN 978-0-545-74615-1

Copyright © 2011 by Edizioni Piemme S.p.A., Corso Como 15, 20154 Milan, Italy.

International Rights © Atlantyca S.p.A.

English translation © 2015 by Atlantyca S.p.A.

GERONIMO STILTON names, characters, and related indicia are copyright, trademark, and exclusive license of Atlantyca S.p.A. All rights reserved. The moral right of the author has been asserted.

Based on an original idea by Elisabetta Dami.

www.geronimostilton.com

Published by Scholastic Inc., 557 Broadway, New York, NY 10012. SCHOLASTIC and associated logos are trademarks and/or registered trademarks of Scholastic Inc.

Stilton is the name of a famous English cheese. It is a registered trademark of the Stilton Cheese Makers' Association. For more information, go to www.stiltoncheese.com.

Text by Geronimo Stilton
Original title Settimo Viaggio nel Regno della Fantasia
Cover by Danilo Barozzi
Illustrations by Danilo Barozzi, Silvia Bigolin, Carla De Bernardi, Federico Brusco, and Piemme's Archives. Color by Christian Aliprandi
Graphics by Chiara Cebraro and Yuko Egusa

Special thanks to Kathryn Cristaldi
Translated by Emily Clement
Interior design by Kevin Callahan / BNGO Books

12 11 10 9 8 7 6 5 4 3 2   15 16 17 18 19/0

Printed in Singapore   46

First printing, June 2015

The Guardians of the Seven Charms

Many centuries ago, Queen Blossom entrusted seven powerful charms to seven guardians:

Coraline

I am the headmistress of Coral Academy, the Underwater Fairy School. I am kind but firm. I expect my students to swim to the top of the class!

Tessa

I am a giant tortoise from the Desert of Eyes and Ears. I am also called the Wise Shelled One and She Who Is Never in One Place. Can you guess why?

Firebeard

I am the head gnome of the village of the Red-nosed Gnomes. Do you like apple juice? We make the tastiest apple juice in the entire Kingdom of Fantasy!

Blizzard

I am a wolf with pure white fur who lives in the Realm of the Towering Peaks. I am searching for one special mouse . . .

Crystal

I am a nightingale with a body made of shimmering crystal. I am the guardian of the Gilded Crystal Scale, which measures the purity of a person's heart.

The Maiden of the Tapestry

I am a maiden who lives inside a magical woven tapestry with my faithful unicorn by my side. If you want to visit me, you have to believe in the power of dreams!

Sid

I am a giant squid from the deepest, darkest parts of the ocean. Some say I have cold eyes, but believe me, it's nothing personal.

I LOVE SUMMER IN THE CITY!

It was a **STUNNING** summer night in New Mouse City. The sun was setting, turning the sky a fabumouse shade of **pink**. Oh, how I love summer in the city!

I was heading home after a long day at work, and—oops! Excuse me, I haven't introduced

That's me!

myself. My name is Stilton, *Geronimo Stilton*, and I run *The Rodent's Gazette*, the most popular newspaper on Mouse Island!

Anyway, where was I? Oh, yes, that **evening** I was walking home, feeling peaceful and happy. I decided to treat myself to some ice cream.

Lucky for me, my favorite ice-cream parlor, **Tutti Frutti**, was on

my way. When I arrived I looked at the counter . . .

Holey cheese! So many flavors!

There were at least thirty-four different flavors of **ice cream**! The owner, Lickety Splitz, greeted me.

"Hi, Mr. Stilton! I just read your new **KINGDOM OF FANTASY** book, *The Search for Treasure*. I loved it! I love books with knights and princesses and **gnomes** and dragons and . . ."

I was glad Lickety liked my book, but I have to admit I was having trouble paying attention to him. How could I concentrate with all that **ice cream** staring me in the snout?!

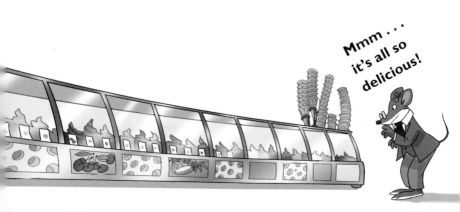

Mmm . . . it's all so delicious!

Still, Lickety didn't seem to notice. "When will you be writing your next *fantasy* book, Mr. Stilton?" he babbled. "And, tell me, where do you get your ideas for these books?"

That got my attention. How do I explain the **KINGDOM OF FANTASY**? "Well, the truth is that each of these books comes from a real adventure," I began.

Lickety's eyes **widened**. "You mean that you've *actually* been to that place?!" he squeaked.

I coughed. I knew it wouldn't be easy to explain, but I tried. "Yes, I really go there, but in **DREAMS**—that is, while I'm dreaming—um, you see, I'm *sleeping*, but then I'm dreaming about the adventure, so . . ." I mumbled.

Lickety looked at me strangely. "So then you don't get there by **plane** or train or bus or anything. You just go to sleep," he squeaked. "Hey, maybe I could go to the **KINGDOM OF FANTASY**, too!"

I nodded. "Um, sure, I guess so," I answered. To be **honest**, I wasn't really sure how I first ended up in the Kingdom of Fantasy. It all started when I found a jewelry box in my attic and then I guess I fell asleep, because I had the *WILDEST* dream. Of course, I don't dream about the Kingdom of Fantasy every time I go to sleep. Sometimes it just sort of happens.

"Remember when you met the **Dragon of the Rainbow** and the time you went to that chocolate castle?" Lickety said.

I smiled, remembering.

I was still thinking about my *exciting* adventures when a voice behind me grumbled, "Hey, you, what's taking so long? Pick a flavor and move on!"

I turned around and realized there was a LONG, LONG line of rodents behind me. Everyone huffed impatiently.

"Hurry up!"

"This isn't **brain surgery**!"

"Any day now . . ."

Oh, how embarrassing!

I was just about to choose any old flavor when I felt someone TUGGING

Remember . . .

It's a magical place!

Hmph!

on my jacket. It was a **SMALL** mouseling holding her mama's paw. "Are you Mr. Geronimo Stilton? The author of the books about the Kingdom of Fantasy? They're my favorite! When are you writing the next one?" she squeaked.

"Well, I—um . . ." I stammered.

Now everyone was really **STARING** at me.

An old rodent with a long handlebar mustache tapped me on the shoulder. "Congratulations, young mouse! I love reading your fantasy books to my grandchildren! They're so much fun!

Are we moving yet?

I want ice cream . . .

I'm turning gray . . .

Come on!

By the way, when are you writing the next Kingdom of Fantasy book?"

I didn't have time to respond before a lady mouse shoved a piece of paper under my nose. "I'd like your autograph, please, and write, 'To Scamper, from Geronimo Stilton'! My son will be so happy! By the way, when are you writing the next adventure?"

A crowd began to gather around me. It seemed everyone had forgotten about the ice cream. Now they just wanted to know one thing: When was I writing the next **KINGDOM OF FANTASY** book?

"Um, w-well . . ." I stuttered.

Lucky for me, Lickety Splitz came to my rescue. He handed me a **humongous** ice-cream cone with a zillion different flavors! I recognized **FOURTEEN** of them.

"Here's hoping that you'll write a new,

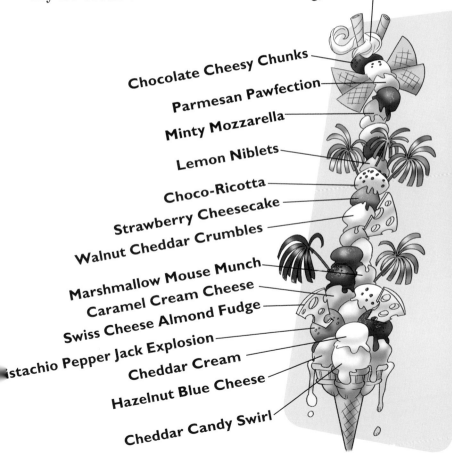

FABUMOUSE fantasy book really soon!" he squeaked.

I thanked everyone and dug into my ice cream.

Dollop of whipped cream on top

Chocolate Cheesy Chunks

Parmesan Pawfection

Minty Mozzarella

Lemon Niblets

Choco-Ricotta

Strawberry Cheesecake

Walnut Cheddar Crumbles

Marshmallow Mouse Munch

Caramel Cream Cheese

Swiss Cheese Almond Fudge

Pistachio Pepper Jack Explosion

Cheddar Cream

Hazelnut Blue Cheese

Cheddar Candy Swirl

DO YOU WANT THE GOOD NEWS OR THE BAD NEWS FIRST?

The next morning, when I reached my office at *The Rodent's Gazette*, I saw that my coworkers and my **family** were all gathered there.

My grandfather, William Shortpaws (founder of *The Rodent's Gazette*), checked his watch and thundered, "Grandson, **YOU'RE LATE**! We've been waiting for you!"

I gulped. Have you ever met my grandfather? He's super TOUGH and always threatening to take back control of the paper.

"I **didn't know** we were having a m-m-meeting," I stammered.

My cousin Trap snickered. "We're having a

meeting about you, Gerry Berry."

Huh? What was he **squeaking** about? And why was everyone *staring* at me? First it happened last night at the ice-cream place, and now at work. I was beginning to get a complex!

"Okay, so do you want to hear the good news or the bad news first?" Trap asked, with a sly smile.

My grandfather grumbled impatiently, "Oh, for rat's sake, just tell him! Come on—before

mold grows on my whiskers. I've got other things to do today!"

My nephew Benjamin took my paw. A *sinking* feeling came over me. What if the bad news was really bad? Like maybe Grandfather William sold the paper. Or my pet fish, *Hannibal*, had gone belly up. Or they stopped making cheddar melts at the Squeak & Chew.

Characters in the Kingdom of Fantasy

I am King Skywings!

Who? Who?

Captain Coldhea at your service!

I'm Boils!

So I said, "I'll take the good news first."

"The **good news** is: Your book *THE SEARCH FOR TREASURE* is a **bestseller**! Readers love it!" Benjamin squeaked.

I smiled. I love my fans!

"The **bad news** is: They love it so much they want a new fantasy book — now," Trap added.

"Grandson, you need to start **WRITING**

immediately!" Grandfather William demanded.

"You mean RIGHT NOW?" I asked.

Oops. Wrong question. Grandfather William began shouting so loud the windows in the office began to RATTLE. "Grandson, are your ears full of cheese? Or maybe you need a dictionary. Of course immediately means now! We need to get the seventh adventure in the Kingdom of Fantasy in print immediately! The deadline was yesterday! You're late!" he thundered.

I wanted to point out that I couldn't have missed a **deadline** if I didn't know it existed, but I didn't want to upset Grandfather. So instead, I tried to explain my writing process.

"Well, you see — the thing is, I can't write it now, because I can write books about the Kingdom of Fantasy only when I have a special dream, and . . ."

My voice trailed off. So much for not **angering** Grandfather. He looked like he was about to hit the ceiling and *shoot* out the roof!

"Special dream? Well, then start *dreaming*, Grandson!" he ordered.

Benjamin brought me a steaming **CUP** of chamomile tea. "Maybe this will help make you sleepy," he offered.

I took a sip, trying to relax. It didn't work. I felt **JUMPIER** than ever. Then everyone left and I lay down on the sofa in my office, placing a **soft pillow** under my head. I closed my eyes, hoping I would **fall** asleep quickly, but . . . I couldn't sleep!

I tried lying on my left side, but it gave me a leg **cramp**. So I tried my right side, but I got a paw **cramp**.

I turned onto my stomach, then onto my back, then upside down.

Still, I couldn't fall asleep!

Rancid rat hairs! I was having a **nightmare**, and I wasn't even dreaming!

I put the pillow over my ears. Then I turned on the air conditioning. A second later I turned off the air conditioning. I tried sipping a warm glass of milk, **nibbling** on a piece of cheese, and reading from the PHONE BOOK.

Finally, I attempted to count sheep, but I kept losing count and having to start all over again.

Nothing worked!

10 STRATEGIES FOR FALLING ASLEEP

I TURNED TO THE RIGHT

AND THE LEFT . . .

. . . ON MY STOMACH . . .

. . . ON MY BACK . . .

. . . COVERING MY EARS

WITH A PILLOW

. . . TRYING AN UNUSUAL POSITION . . .

. . . NIBBLING ON A PIECE OF CHEESE . . .

TIME IS WASTING!

I left the office more stressed out than ever! In fact, I was such a wreck that before I even made it out the door, I . . .

– **BUMPED** into a desk, causing a pile of books to fall on my paw. Ouch!

– collided with a rodent who was drinking a cup of tea, scalding my fur. Double ouch!

– tripped over a wastebasket, frazzling my whiskers. Triple ouch!

By the time I got outside, I was ready to scream! I flew down the street like a madmouse. (Well, okay, I didn't really fly, but you get the picture. I was fast!)

What a terrible day!

When I reached my home at 8 Mouseford Lane I ran right to my bedroom and threw on my favorite pj's. Then I closed the curtains.

I **snuggled** into bed and had just managed to drift off when the telephone RANG.

Ring, ring, riiiing!

I leaped out of bed and grabbed the phone so fast I could have been a contender for the annual **New Mouse City Firemouse Rise-and-Shine Competition**!

My grandfather's voice shrieked in my ear, "Well, did you dream? Did you write anything? Time is wasting!"

My whiskers trembled. "Please, Grandfather. I cannot sleep on **command**, dream on **command**, or write on **command**!" I moaned.

But he had already hung up.

Then I had an **IDEA**. I would try to write my seventh Kingdom of Fantasy book without dreaming. After all, I was an author—I'd just use my imagination.

So I opened the curtains, grabbed my computer, and started the FIRST PAGE of a new

document. I typed: "The Seventh Adventure in the Kingdom of Fantasy, Chapter 1, Page 1."

I stared at the blank page, but nothing came to mind . . . or at least, nothing right. No, those stories were SPECIAL, even if they just came from my dreams. It wouldn't be right to make it up. I sighed and turned off the computer.

I was still debating what to do next when I heard the RINGTONE of my cell phone. I had received a text message. It was from Benjamin.

I called him right away and told him how I still needed to FALL ASLEEP so I could dream.

That's when Benjamin suggested I go to the beach. No, not to build sand castles and go bodysurfing. Actually, I've never been **bodysurfing**, except for the time I got hit by a **giant wave** and ended up on a pile of rocks!

"I'm going to the beach to play with my friends. Why don't you come? You can relax," he suggested.

A little while later we arrived at the best beach in New Mouse City, **Pink Seashell Beach**.

While Benjamin played with his friends, I sat on my beach chair in the **shade**. The sun was high in the sky, and the air was suffocating.

Oh, who goes to the beach to relax in the middle of the **sweltering** summer? A desperate

mouse, that's who! And now I was not only desperate, I was also dripping with sweat!

Still, the minute I closed my eyes, I found myself in a magical vortex of stars . . .

CRYSTAL
PLANET

The Kingdom of Fantasy

The Kingdom of Fantasy is endless
because the imagination is endless!
Anyone who can dream can explore
it and discover even more new
kingdoms within it.

MYSTERIOUS
ABYSS

CASTLE OF
DREAMS

KINGDOM
OF THE PIX

KINGDOM OF THE
FIRE DRAGONS

KINGDOM OF
THE FAIRIES

LAND OF
NIGHTMARES

CITY OF TH
BLUE UNICOR

LAND OF
TROLLS

KINGDOM
OF THE
WITCHES

KINGDOM
OF THE
DIGGERTS

KINGDOM OF
THE SEA

DESERT OF
EYES AND
EARS

KINGDOM OF
THE GNOMES

TALKING
FOREST

RAINBOW VALLEY

KINGDOM OF
THE SILVER
DRAGONS

REALM OF THE
TOWERING
PEAKS

KINGDOM OF
THE ELVES

KINGDOM
OF THE
NORTHERN
GIANTS

LAND OF THE
OGRES

N
W   E
S

COME ON,
MOVE YOUR TAIL!

Suddenly, I felt a pinch on my ear, and a voice squealed, "Hey, you! Whoosy Whatsy, I mean, SIR KNIGHT, wake up!"

I opened my eyes and saw a hermit crab peering out from beneath a large purple shell.

Wake up!

Wh-who's there?!?

He looked at me with round, **bulging eyes** and an impatient expression. When I didn't respond he quickly reached out and pinched my other ear.

"**OW!**" I squeaked.

"Oh, good, now we're getting somewhere," he said. "Come on, Your Knightliness, we have to **whatchamacallit**—get the show on the road, shake a tail, get those paws *pumping!*"

I sat up, shocked, and looked around. "Who are you? And, why are you talking? **Crabs** don't talk!" I yelped.

He **pinched** my snout, clearly offended.

"Who are you, Professor of Crabology? Who says we don't talk?" he cried, **STRUTTING** in front of me, showing off his shell with an air of importance.

"For your information, I'm not just any old crab!

31

I am the whatsitcalled for **whatsherface!**" he declared.

"Huh?" I said, scratching my head.

"I mean," he continued, "I am the **MESSENGER** for Her Royal Majesty, the One Responsible for Imperative Reporting, the Main Mouthpiece of Messages, **HE WHO KNOWS WHAT NO ONE ELSE MAY** (except you, me, and Those Who Defend the Mystery of the Chain of the Seven Charms), the Crab of All Crabs, the Crustacean of All Crustaceans. That is, I am **Chatterclaws of the Seven Seas!**" Then he bowed and added, "Welcome to the **KINGDOM OF FANTASY** — or rather, welcome back!"

He showed me a gold medallion with the portrait of the **BEAUTIFUL** fairy Blossom on one side.

Do you know **Blossom**? She is the incredibly kind and caring Queen of the Fairies. On my first visit to the Kingdom of Fantasy I pledged my loyalty to her.

On the other side of the medallion was a portrait of **Chatterclaws** and a message in the Fantasian Alphabet.* Can you translate it?

* You can find the Fantasian Alphabet on page 310.

Chatterclaws of the Seven Seas

Chatterclaws

Ancestry: Chatterclaws is of the Crustacean dynasty, descending from the famous Blabberclaws, the renowned Marine Messenger originally chosen by Blossom to carry her secret messages through the waters of the Seven Seas of the Kingdom of Fantasy.

Home: He inherited the Blabberhouse (which he now calls the Chatterhouse), the seashell in which he lives. This magical shell contains a complete wardrobe with every possible outfit and even a compartment filled with secret surprises. (Shhh!)

What Makes Him Special: He's very friendly and knows many fish all over the sea.

Personality: Chatterclaws loves to chat and is a good messenger, but he often forgets whatchamacallits — or, er, words.

His Secret: Chatterclaws is in love with fellow hermit crab Classyclaws and is planning on proposing to her soon. (But don't tell anyone!)

Classyclaws

The medallion read: Chatterclaws, Mythical Marine Messenger.

I realized that the medallion was a badge of honor given to the crab by Blossom. Wow! For a small hermit crab, Chatterclaws sure had a **BIG** job. Now if he could just lay off the pinching . . .

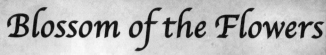

Blossom of the Flowers

White Queen, Lady of Peace and Happiness, She Who Brings World Harmony, Queen of the Fairies, and the Heart of the Kingdom of Fantasy

Blossom lives in the Crystal Castle, an extraordinary palace made entirely of pure crystal.

Sir Geronimo of Stilton has helped Blossom and the Kingdom of Fantasy six times. The first time, he awakened the queen from an enchanted sleep; the second time, he helped her find the Heart of Happiness; the third time, he freed her from the villain who had kidnapped her; the fourth time, he saved the last dragon egg; the fifth time, he stopped earthquakes from destroying the Kingdom of Fantasy; and the sixth time, he fulfilled the Ancient Gemstone Prophecy.

MESSAGE FROM BLOSSOM OF THE FLOWERS!

I was still thinking about Chatterclaws's important position when he pinched me on the tail. Oh, why do crabs have such sharp claws?

"Okay, listen up, Sir Knight!" he declared, ignoring my CRY of pain. "I am here to deliver a very special thingamabob—I mean, whatchamacallit—I mean, **message** from the queen."

Then he cleared his throat, coughed, GARGLED with seawater, and **PROCLAIMED**, *"Message from Blossom of the Flowers for Sir Geronimo of Stilton, entrusted to the Mythical Marine Messenger, Chatterclaws of the Crustaceans!"*

The crab interrupted himself and pointed

Message from Blossom!

with one of his claws. "That's me!"

Then he continued. *"I, Blossom of the Flowers, welcome you back to our kingdom. The mission I need you to complete this time will be difficult, risky, and very dangerous, for you must face the* wicked **Wizard of the Black Pearl***!"*

At this, the crab stopped and ***shivered***, adding, "If you ask me, you should say your good-byes now. No one beats the wizard."

Then he went on, *"Through a spell, this wicked wizard was trapped for a thousand years in a* **watery** *prison, at the bottom of the Mysterious Abyss. But now the wizard is* **free***!"*

I began to **GNAW** my whiskers. A wicked wizard on the loose? Say my good-byes? Oh, how did I get myself into these messes?

I was such a NeRVºUS wreck that it took

all of my willpower to concentrate on what Chatterclaws was saying next.

Long story short, it turned out the WICKED wizard had an *evil* plan to use his power to take over the entire Kingdom of Fantasy.

"Your mission will be to find the **seven enchanted charms** given by Blossom to seven separate guardians. When the charms are strung together on the GOLDEN CHAIN and returned to Blossom, peace will reign. Well, what do you say, Sir Geronimo of Stilton? Do you accept the mission?" the crab finished.

But before I could reply, Chatterclaws DISAPPEARED into his shell!

Huh?

A minute later he reemerged, holding a strange seashell-shaped telephone. It was the CHATTERPHONE.

Rinnng!

CHATTERPHONE

Wizard of the Black Pearl

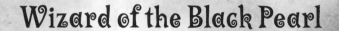

The All-Terrifying, the Swallower of Hopes, the Ruler of Darkness, of the dynasty of Warlocks of the Night

Descendent of the Dark Wizards, he is a very powerful and evil sorcerer. He is greedy for power and tried to control the entire Kingdom of Fantasy a thousand years ago. He was defeated by Blossom and her allies, and was imprisoned for a millennium in the Mysterious Abyss. But during his long imprisonment, he formed an alliance with the wicked Oyster People, who gave him all the pearls produced in the Seven Seas. Now, a thousand years later, he is using his wealth and magical powers to try to take control of the kingdom once again.

Queen Blossom was on the line. "Knight, if you accept this mission, the first charm and the *golden chain* are guarded by Coraline. But be careful, the Wizard of the Black Pearl has **DANGEROUS** allies and spies everywhere!" she warned.

I was scared, but how could I say no to the queen?

As soon as I accepted, Chatterclaws grabbed the phone and hung up.

"Sorry, but these long-distance calls cost more than my five-year subscription to **Crustacean Nation**!" he complained.

The crab turned to leave but then suddenly **slapped** a claw against his forehead. "Jumping jellyfish, I almost forgot. You need your thingamajig—I mean, your **SEA ARMOR**! Follow me!" he called, disappearing once again into his shell.

A moment later, I found myself in the most amazing place. Chatterclaws's seashell was actually a *luxurious* apartment!

The crab opened the lid of a large wooden box and said solemnly, "For you."

Inside the box I found a suit of armor made of **RED** coral, with a cape made of **woven** seaweed. There was also a sword, a small bag, and a **GOLD** ring with Blossom's seal. A piece of parchment read:

"I, Blossom of the Flowers, name you the Knight of the Seven Seas, with power below and above the waves and the authority to speak in my name!"

SEA ARMOR

THE ARMOR OF THE KNIGHT OF THE SEVEN SEAS

Cloak made of woven seaweed, and coral pin

Sea armor made of red coral

Sword with a hilt in the shape of a red starfish

Gold ring with the seal of Blossom: a blue flower

I, Blossom of the Flowers, name you the Knight of the Seven Seas, with power below and above the waves and the authority to speak in my name!

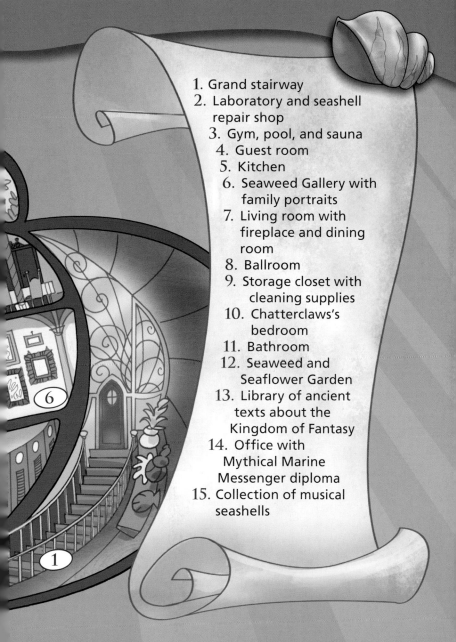

1. Grand stairway
2. Laboratory and seashell repair shop
3. Gym, pool, and sauna
4. Guest room
5. Kitchen
6. Seaweed Gallery with family portraits
7. Living room with fireplace and dining room
8. Ballroom
9. Storage closet with cleaning supplies
10. Chatterclaws's bedroom
11. Bathroom
12. Seaweed and Seaflower Garden
13. Library of ancient texts about the Kingdom of Fantasy
14. Office with Mythical Marine Messenger diploma
15. Collection of musical seashells

GOOD-BYE AND SEE YA!

A little later we left the Chatterhouse and the crab gave me the list of the *seven charms* written on a strip of seaweed. Then he pinched me on the ear again (if only I had worn **earmuffs**!) and said, "Okay, Whatsyourname, good-bye and see ya! Also, my **condolences**, since you probably won't make it back alive . . ."

As he began **skittering** toward the sea, I ran after him. "Hey, **WAIT**! Aren't you going to come with me?" I cried nervously.

The crab shook his head. "I'm a message carrier, not a **BABYSITTER**. No, thank goodness, my mission is over. If you kick the bucket, it's not my problem," he muttered.

THE SEVEN ENCHANTED CHARMS

1. The Coral Heart

Guarded by Coraline at Coral Academy. It's a symbol of love and has the power to reveal how much love is in a person's heart.

2. The Clasping Hands

Guarded by She Who Is Never in One Place in the Desert of Eyes and Ears. It's a symbol of friendship. Whoever holds it will know how to give and receive help from friends.

3. The Medallion of the Sun and the Moon

Guarded by the leader of the Red-nosed Gnomes in Rainbow Valley. It has the power to stretch the night and lengthen the day.

4. The Diamond Star

Guarded by Blizzard, a ferocious white wolf, in the Realm of the Towering Peaks. It's a symbol of courage . . . and to win it, one must demonstrate great courage!

5. The Crystal Feather

Guarded by Crystal, the nightingale in the Realm of the Starry Sky, on the Crystal Planet. It can be won only by one with a pure heart.

6. The Silver Unicorn

Guarded by the Maiden of the Tapestry and her unicorn in the Castle of Dreams. Only one who knows the importance of dreams and the power of imagination can win this charm.

7. The Golden Pearl

Guarded by Sid the Giant Squid, also known as the One with Many Arms, in the Cave of the Deepest Darkness. It has the power to grant wishes to whoever possesses it.

It was a very dangerous mission!

KNIGHT OF THE SEVEN SEAS

I chewed my whiskers to keep from **bursting** into tears of terror.

"To be honest," Chatterclaws went on, "I'm surprised you're still alive. As soon as the Wizard of the Black Pearl finds out about your mission, he'll **HUNT** you down until there's nothing left of you but a headstone with your name on it. But don't worry; I'll bring fresh **flowers** every day."

Before I could faint, the Chatterphone **rang**. Maybe it was Blossom again, saying she had made a mistake! Maybe my mission was actually to travel to the Kingdom of Fantasy Resort and Spa. I pictured myself lounging by a pool, sipping a **cheese smoothie**.

"Uh-huh, yep, no problem. Will do, Your

Majesty." Chatterclaws's voice **interrupted** my thoughts. He spoke to the caller for a few moments, then hung up and turned to me.

"Well, Knight, it's your lucky day. Blossom is sending me with you. The first charm is guarded by Coraline **underwater** in the Kingdom of the Sea."

I let out a sigh of relief. "So, how do we get there? I don't remember . . ."

Chatterclaws **rolled** his eyes, grumbling, "Must I do everything? We call a TAXI, of course!"

TUNA CAB: THE FISH TAXI

He knows all the secrets of undersea traffic: whale traffic patterns, hot and cold currents, obstacles, drops, coral reefs, refueling stations, and—most important—he knows how to avoid areas swarming with sharks!

He let out a whistle, and a moment later an **ENORMOUSE** tuna arrived, fully equipped with seats for its passengers.

Chatterclaws jumped on board and cried, "To the **Kingdom of the Sea**, please!"

Then, turning, he said, "Well, what are you doing? Waiting for algae to grow under your paws?"

I jumped on board and fastened my seat belt. The tuna cab took off like a shot and . . .

1. We plunged into the sea like a rocket!

2. We almost smashed into some massive rocks!

3. We got **TOSSED** around in a strong ocean current like socks in a clothes dryer!

I want to get offfff!

Rats! Did I mention I'm afraid of boats and I'm prone to seasickness?

Anyway, where was I? Oh, right, after about a **MILLION** years, the tuna stopped, checked his meter, and announced, "We're here! That'll be thirty-four clams! And don't forget the **TIP**!"

The Kingdom of the Sea

THE SEARCH FOR THE CORAL HEART

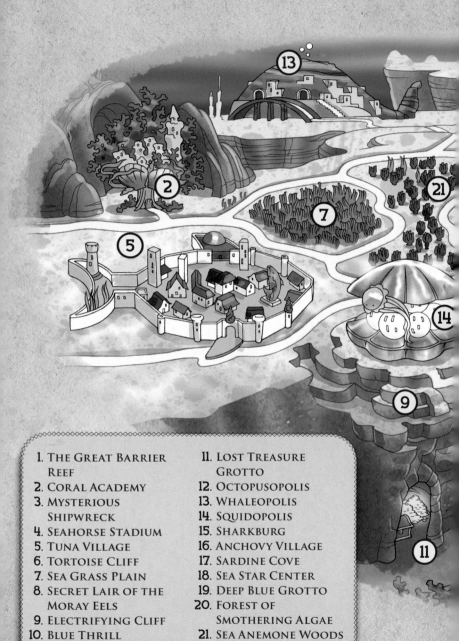

The Kingdom of the Sea

OF COURSE, WE'RE THE PLUMBERS!

Chatterclaws disappeared into the Chatterhouse and reemerged a few moments later with a pile of **seashells**.

"Call if you need another pickup," the tuna called over his fin before he **zipped** off.

Soon we were standing in front of the magnificent **CORAL ACADEMY**, where Coraline* was waiting for us. "Ah, you're the plumbers, right? And you're here to repair the **leaky** faucet, right?" she proclaimed with a wink.

Then she whispered, "The **Wizard of the Black Pearl** has ᛋᑭᛁᛂᛋ everywhere. I know why you're here. Follow me."

The crab nodded to the queen and replied in a **LOUD** voice, "Yes, of course, we're the

*Geronimo met Coraline in his book *The Search for Treasure.*

$plumbers$!" Then he produced a plumber's uniform from his shell. "Go on, Sir Whoosy Whatsy," he whispered. "Put this on over your

armor and **PRETEND** to be a plumber!"

I had no idea how to pretend to be a plumber, but what could I do? I didn't want the wizard's **SPIES** to find us. A minute later, dressed in **blue** overalls and a matching hat, I mumbled, "Um, don't worry, ma'am, we *plumbers* know how to, um, plumb anything. Show us the bathroom and we'll start, er, plumbing!"

Coraline led us down the long, colorful hallways of Coral Academy. As I remembered from my previous journey, the **CORRIDORS** were full of little *fairies* chatting and laughing as they headed to their classrooms. Some whispered and smiled as the headmistress *floated* by, but no one seemed to notice us.

We had fooled them all into thinking we were real plumbers!

When we reached the bathroom, Coraline stopped and, after giving us a look, tossed a

shimmering powder into the air and whispered a fairy spell:

"May our doubles continue to appear, while we simply disappear!"

Fairy magic!

A moment later, we SPLIT in two! Yep, I am not pulling your paw! Before our very eyes were exact copies of me, Chatterclaws, and Coraline. Our look-alikes strode into the bathroom, while we, the real us, became as TRANSPARENT as thin air.

Follow me . . .

Aha!

It was then that I noticed a fairy wearing a necklace of **SHINING** pearls hiding behind a column, **SPYING** on our doubles. When our doubles went into the bathroom, the fairy followed.

Quickly, Coraline motioned us into the **LIBRARY**.

WHAT TRAITORS, THOSE OYSTERS!

The fairy entered the library, lit three candles in a gold *candelabra*, and examined every corner of the room.

Meanwhile, Chatterclaws and I took off our plumber **disguises** and soon became **visible** again. I was happy to see myself. I admit it, I missed my own **fur**!

Coral Academy's library was an amazing place. Besides spectacular high VAULTED ceilings, the walls were covered with books of all kinds, **COLORS**, and sizes. I glanced at the titles, such as: *One, Two, Three, Poof!: The Fairies' Guide to Magic Potions; How Do You Spell Magic?; Easy Spells for First-Year Fairies; Wands and Wings for Beginners.*

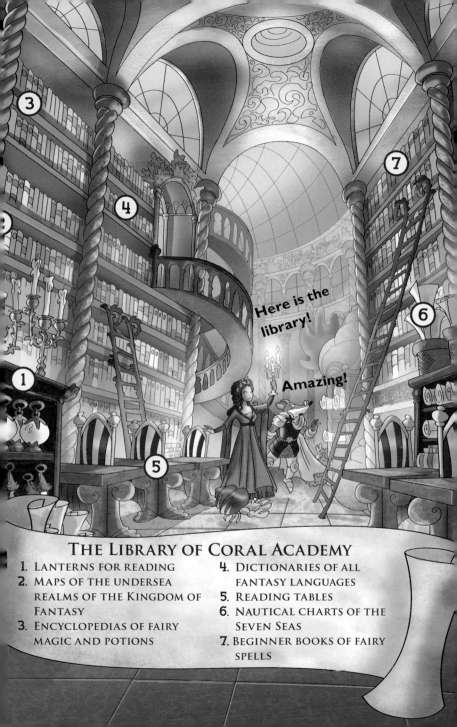

Here is the library!

Amazing!

THE LIBRARY OF CORAL ACADEMY

1. LANTERNS FOR READING
2. MAPS OF THE UNDERSEA REALMS OF THE KINGDOM OF FANTASY
3. ENCYCLOPEDIAS OF FAIRY MAGIC AND POTIONS
4. DICTIONARIES OF ALL FANTASY LANGUAGES
5. READING TABLES
6. NAUTICAL CHARTS OF THE SEVEN SEAS
7. BEGINNER BOOKS OF FAIRY SPELLS

I was so busy reading the book titles, I didn't realize Coraline had finished searching the room for **SPIES** until she tapped me on the shoulder. Startled, I **JUMPED** a foot in the air. Oh, how embarrassing!

"Now you understand the **reason** for all the precautions, right, Sir Knight?" she asked. "The Wizard of the Black Pearl has **spies** everywhere. During the thousand years he was held prisoner in the Mysterious Abyss, he allied himself with the Oyster People. In exchange for **Power**, they've given him all the pearls produced in the Seven Seas of the Kingdom of Fantasy."

Chatterclaws snorted. "What **traitors**, those oysters!"

The fairy nodded, adding, "The wizard pays his spies with pearls. Did you notice the pearl necklace on the fairy **spying** on us? Evidently, she has met the wizard."

Coraline sighed but then shook her head. "Okay, enough with these **SAD** thoughts," she continued brightly. "If you've managed to make it all the way here, it means your **MISSION** has begun well!"

Then she turned to me. "Knight, I will give you the **FiRST CHARM**. It was entrusted to me centuries and centuries ago by Blossom herself. Our queen feared that one day some *villain* could use the enormous power of the seven charms for evil purposes. So she sent each charm to a loyal guardian in many different parts of the Kingdom of Fantasy."

Then she added, proudly, "I am the guardian of the first charm: the **Coral Heart**. It is a small heart made of red coral, and a symbol of the love that we must have for all—friends or enemies."

The fairy pointed to a thick **RED** book high on a shelf. "Can you please retrieve that book, Sir Knight? The **HeaRt** is inside," she said.

"Um, of course," I mumbled, even though my paws shook. No, I wasn't afraid of the Heart. I was afraid of climbing up the TALL ladder to reach the book! Did I mention I'm afraid of heights?

Luckily, I managed to get the book without **breaking** my tail. Whew!

The book was called *Love: It Makes the World Go Round (and Up, and Down, and Sideways!)*. I opened it, and inside, I found the **small red** Coral Heart.

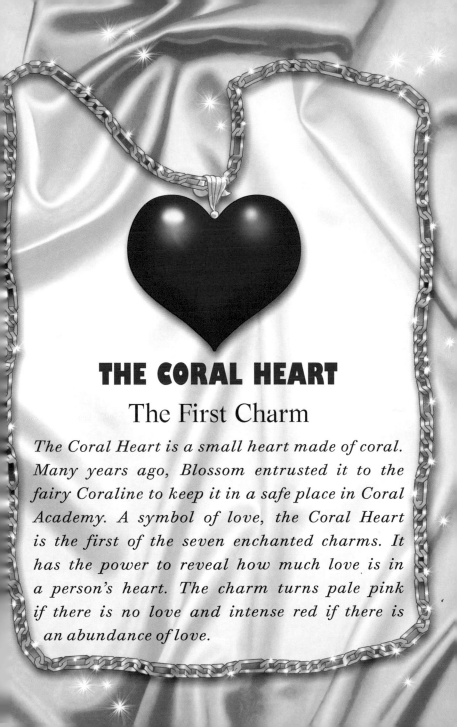

THE CORAL HEART
The First Charm

The Coral Heart is a small heart made of coral. Many years ago, Blossom entrusted it to the fairy Coraline to keep it in a safe place in Coral Academy. A symbol of love, the Coral Heart is the first of the seven enchanted charms. It has the power to reveal how much love is in a person's heart. The charm turns pale pink if there is no love and intense red if there is an abundance of love.

DON'T WORRY

"I promise to **GUARD** this heart with my life," I told Coraline, removing the **Coral Heart** and the golden chain from the book with a grin.

I must say, I was starting to feel pretty good about this mission. After all, it hadn't been that difficult to find the first *enchanted charm*. And, well, except for that scary ride in the tuna cab and climbing up that *super-high* ladder, overall, I would give myself an A+ on my accomplishments so far.

Still, before I could get carried away and attempt to pat myself on my own back, Coraline gave me a **WARM** hug and a **serious** warning. Rats! I knew things were going too *smoothly* on this adventure!

"Watch out, Knight!" the fairy warned. "It won't be easy to find the next six charms. You will face grave dangers, because the **Wizard of the Black Pearl** is after you. And when you meet the next guardians, you must pass very **difficult** tests to prove you really are the Knight of the Seven Seas. Otherwise, they may **refuse** to give you the charms . . . after all, they've had them for a long time. And finally, once you've obtained the charms, you must make sure they are not **stolen** by the wizard's spies."

By the time Coraline was finished, I felt like **crawling** into a cave and hibernating for a year! Too bad mice don't **hibernate**. Who wouldn't want a nice long rest?

Instead, I gulped.

Gulp!

I wanted to **cry**, but I didn't have a tissue. Plus, I

The Ten Levels of Despair for Sir Geronimo of Stilton

1. Wow, everything's going great!

2. It's going to be great—I can feel it.

3. It's going good.

4. It's going okay.

5. Um . . . who knows what will happen?

6. Maybe it's not as easy as I thought . . .

7. It's not going to be easy . . .

8. Uh-oh—it's going to be difficult . . .

9. Um, this is really difficult!

10. Rats! I'll never be able to do

always did my best to finish every mission. I had to keep going, even if I was scared out of my fur!

"Don't worry," Coraline **COMFORTED** me. "Each charm will help you on your mission, because each one has a power. As I said, the Coral Heart has the power to reveal how much love is in a person's heart."

Right then I realized the Heart had a **MESSAGE** written on it in the Fantasian Alphabet.* Can you translate it?

* You can find the Fantasian Alphabet on page 310.

I translated it. *"Love conquers all!"* I read out loud.

Just then Chatterclaws pinched my tail with a claw, making me JUMP.

"Come on, let's go! The whatchamacallit, I mean, the octoballoon is waiting for us!"

Before I could ask what an octoballoon was, something tapped me on the shoulder.
TAP, TAP!

I turned and saw an enormouse **purple** octopus, with enormouse bulging eyes and long

Wait, who . . . ?

Come on, let's go!

tentacles with enormouse suckers. And one of those **ENORMOUSE** tentacles was what had tapped me on the shoulder! Cheese niblets!

I had barely put the GOLDEN CHAIN around my neck and attached the first charm when Chatterclaws pushed me into a wicker basket held by the octopus. A moment later we took off, heading for the surface of the sea.

UP, UP, UP!

As we climbed, the water became clearer and clearer until we reached the surface of the ocean. Then we burst from the water, popping up into the **sunlight** with a giant SPLASH!

Before I could ask, "How do we reach the shore?" the octopus began to push us toward the beach.

The wicker basket hit the shore, and I ROLLED out onto the WET sand, over a hard mound of shells, and all the way into a tall pointy cactus. Ouch!

Chatterclaws stepped out of the basket and snorted. "Seriously, Knight? Was that *really* necessary? Come on, I didn't come all the way to the Desert of Eyes and Ears to play games. We're here to find the Clasping Hands, the next enchanted charm, and it won't be easy. It's held by a guardian no one's ever seen."

I stared at the empty, SANDY desert. What a dreary place!

Just then the crab whispered, "Let's go into the Chatterhouse. I must speak with you **ALONE**!"

"But we *are* alone," I said, confused.

Chatterclaws shook his head. "Come on, get with the program, Sir Knight," he whispered. "Remember what Coraline told us: Don't be fooled by appearances. Well, that's what I'm talking about. Even here, the Wizard of the Black Pearl has hidden spies. Who

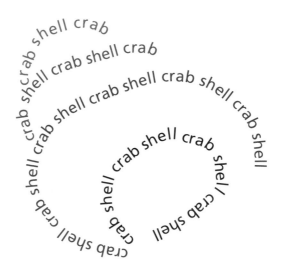

knows who might be listening to us? Now, follow me . . ."

And with that, he *disappeared* into the Chatterhouse.

shell crab shell crab shell crab shell crab shell crab shell crab shell crab shell crab shell crab shell crab shell crab shell crab shell crab shell crab shell crab shell crab shell crab shell crab shell crab shell crab

1. THE STUMBLING TRAIL
2. THE CANYON OF FIERY WINDS
3. THE PETRIFIED BONE MOUNTAINS
4. MOUNT SKULL
5. PARCHED PLAIN
6. THE ROAD TO NOWHERE
7. VACANT VALLEY
8. THE FIELD OF THORNS
9. THE STONE GIANT ARENA
10. THE PLAIN OF THE LOST

WIPE YOUR PAWS
ON THE MAT

As soon as I stepped into the crab shell, Chatterclaws called out, "Wipe your **paws** on the mat, okay? And remember to be careful on the stairs! They're steep. And don't slip, I just waxed the floor!"

I **WIPED** my paws on the mat, was careful on the stairs, and didn't slip on the floor, but my tail got hooked on the coatrack, and it **CRASHED** over.

The crab sighed, then **pushed** me toward a table and chairs. "Sit there and don't move!" he ordered, scuttling off to the kitchen.

When he returned he handed me a glass of **yellow** liquid with a straw and a little umbrella in it.

I was worried that the drink might be some weird fish-flavored concoction, but I didn't want to be rude, so I took a tiny sip. "It's LEMONADE!" I cried, shocked.

"What did you expect, clam bile?" Chatterclaws snorted. Then he stuck a map of the Desert of Eyes and Ears under my nose and said, "We need to study this thingamajig. There are tons of **spies** around."

"So that's how the **DESERT** got its name!" I cried.

"Hmm, maybe there's hope for you yet," the crab commented drily. "Anyway," he continued. "I've got an idea. We can communicate in **secret code** so no spies will understand us. I'll teach it to you."

Then he **PINCHED** my snout, made faces, smacked my head, and shouted meaningless phrases in my ears. What a nightmare!

CHATTERCLAWS'S SECRET CODE

Ow!

When I smack your skull with my claw, it means "someone's listening"!

Huh?!

When I pinch your snout, it means "exactly what I said"!

Ouchie!

When I make a face at you, it means "the opposite of what I said"!

When I shout "careful!" it means "everything's going well"!

Careful!

What?

Everything's great!

What?

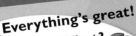

When I say "everything's great!" it means "danger ahead"!

"Now let's practice!" he cried, **SMACKING** me on the head with a claw.

"Um . . . someone's listening?"

"Well done, Sir Knight!" he said.

But then the crab shouted, "Careful!" I looked around, **WORRIED**, because I didn't remember that it actually meant "everything's going well." Cheese and crackers!

"Don't worry. We'll be okay," Chatterclaws said **CONFIDENTLY** as we left the Chatterhouse a few minutes later.

I feel like we're being watched . . .

Just act natural!

The scorching sun greeted us outside, and the sand **burned** my paws. The landscape was harsh and *ROCKY*.

Even worse, I constantly felt as though I was being watched. Were there really spies all around us? Once, I even tripped on a rock that seemed to have been suspiciously moved to make me fall! We **stumbled** along the Stumbling Trail. **OW, OW, OW!** Then we continued through the Canyon of Fiery Winds. Smokin' Swiss bits! Oh, where was a **FIRE EXTINGUISHER**

when you needed one?!

Next we crossed the Petrified Bone Mountains. Were they the **bones** of unlucky travelers? Gulp! We scaled Mount Skull, a **STEEP** mountain shaped like a giant—you guessed it—skull. Double gulp! Finally, we reached the **Road to Nowhere**.

Don't quit!

So tired . . .

The road led to the **heart of the desert**, a place so isolated that there were **no** trees, **no** lakes, and **no** living creatures. Where else would a Road to Nowhere lead? In fact, the area was called **VACANT VALLEY**. Seriously, I couldn't make this stuff up!

That night I fell into a **deep** sleep filled with nightmares. I woke at **dawn**, exhausted and worried. *Take deep breaths*, I told myself. But the air was so hot, I nearly BURNED the inside of my nostrils!

WHOOO DAAARES TO CHAAALLENGE MEEE?

We continued walking until we arrived at a vast stretch of sand and rocks, with clusters of round, **thorny** bushes.

"It looks like we're in the Field of Thingamabobs, I mean the **Field of Thorns**! Start running or you'll never run again!" Chatterclaws warned me.

Just then the wind picked up and I heard an angry whisper: **"Whooo daaares to chaaallenge meee?"**

My teeth began to chatter. It had to be the guardian of the second enchanted charm! He or she was testing me. The **thorny** bushes started chasing me, and I began running as fast as I could. Rancid rat hairs! Who would have guessed **SHRUBBERY** could be so evil!

With a terrific leap, I landed on a rocky ledge where the thorny bushes couldn't reach me.

Heeeelp!

Don't look behind you!

Whew! I was safe by a whisker!
I wanted to rest, but Chatterclaws kept moving. After hours of walking, we arrived at an **ENORMOUSE** clearing as large as a stadium, set off by high rocky walls. It was the **STONE GIANT ARENA**.

Right then the rocks began rolling in the middle of the arena, and little by little they formed something that resembled a **MONSTROUS WARRIOR** made of stone! A round boulder placed itself at the top of the monster, forming its head. Then the warrior turned toward me and thundered, **"Whooo daaares to chaaallenge meee?"**

As if I hadn't guessed, Chatterclaws yelled, "It's another test, Knight! Don't think about how big and **STRONG** he is and how little and **weak** you are, and don't think about how he is a warrior who is used to fighting and you're just a

Whooo daaares to chaaallenge meee?
I want to live!
That rock is ready to roll!

You won't escape me!

scholar with **puny** muscles!" The monster rumbled toward me with steps that made the ground tremble, and I fled, squeaking, "I want to live!" Just then, the crab produced a rope from his shell and lassoed a **CACTUS**

I've got it!

sticking up on the other side of the path.

As the monster took a step forward, Chatterclaws pulled the rope taut. The monster TRIPPED!

For one terrifying second, the immense **stone giant** loomed over me, but right at the last moment, I managed to jump to one side. The giant fell to the ground, **exploding** into a thousand stones.

Heeelp!

Before I could even thank the crab, another voice roared, **"Whooo daaares to chaaallenge meee?"**

Seriously? Couldn't a mouse catch a break?

I raised my snout to the sky, and the scene in front of me made my jaw **drop**.

I realized that the voice was coming from a terrifying **tornado**! The sand swirled in a **spiral** that grew bigger and bigger until the **VORTEX** took the shape of a face with a wide-open mouth and **MENACING** eyes.

Before I could move, the mouth started to close and a swirl of sand surrounded me, **blinding** me. But just then Chatterclaws threw open the door of his *shell* and shouted, "Get in here if you want to live!"

I jumped inside, and he closed the door behind me.

Whew! I was safe by a whisker!

Outside, the **sand storm** raged on, but inside, we were safe.

The crab **SWEPT** up the grains of sand that I'd trekked in, muttering, "You forgot to wipe your paws . . ."

Yep, that crab was a cleaning fanatic!

You forgot to wipe your paws!

WATER! WATER! WATER!

We waited a long while in the Chatterhouse until the wind stopped **HOWLING**, the sand stopped **SWIRLING**, and the storm stopped **raging**. Once there was silence, we peeked outside. What a sight! The **SAND** from the storm had covered *everything*, and we couldn't tell which direction was which. We started to wander under the **BURNING** sun, getting even more tired and discouraged by the minute.

When Chatterclaws finished all the water from inside his house he **burst** into tears. He cried so hard I let him drink the **WATER** in my canteen.

What can I say? It's hard to watch a sea creature cry.

"Thanks!" the crab said, **guzzling** the precious liquid.

Finally, we decided to rest in the **shade** of a rock sticking up out of the sand. Even though we were in the shade, my fur still felt like it was on **fire**. It was soooo **HOT**!

I closed my eyes and tried to pretend I was somewhere else . . . relaxing by a **BABBLING** brook, splashing in the water at **LaKe Peaceful Paws** . . . But when I opened my eyes all I saw was a hot desert. Ugh!

I was about to drink the last drop of water from my canteen when I noticed a plant in front of me. Just looking at it told me that it was thirstier than I was. Its stem was drooping, its leaves were **shriveled**, and the flower sprouting at the top was **wilted**. Filled with pity, I poured the last

drop of water onto the plant. To my surprise, little by little, the plant started to recover!

It was then that I heard a strange murmuring. It sounded like a **WHISPER** coming from the soil! The whisper was like a chorus of *thousands* of tiny voices, murmuring together:

"CONGRATULATIONS! YOU'VE PASSED MY TEST:
THE BUSHES, THE STONE GIANT, AND ALL THE REST.
NOW I WILL HELP YOU ON YOUR WAY.
SO LISTEN CLOSELY TO WHAT I SAY . . ."

I realized that the voices were coming from all the grains of **SAND** that made up the desert.

Talking sand, aggressive stone giants . . . what was next, *DANCING* cacti? I pinched myself to make sure I wasn't hallucinating from the heat.

Then Chatterclaws explained, "It's the **GUARDIAN** of the second charm!"

A moment later the voices continued:

**"To find the second charm,
no need to look around.
The answer is beneath you:
It's right here in the ground!"**

Suddenly, the soil beneath us started to **Rise**, and we rose along with it. Up, up, up we climbed into the air. When I looked down I realized we were now standing on the head of an enormouse *green tortoise*!

The tortoise opened her mouth and **yawned** so deeply we practically crashed to the ground.

Then she said in a **GROGGY** voice, "Who has awakened the guardian of the second charm from her hundred-year sleep?"

Wow—a hundred years! Talk about a **DEEP SLEEP**! I mean, don't get me wrong, I love catching a few **Zzz's** as much as the next rodent, but one hundred years really takes the cheesecake!

Anyway, where was I? Oh, yes. I quickly showed the tortoise the ring with Blossom's symbol and explained that I was searching for the seven charms.

The tortoise stared at me. "You are an adventurer with great **courage** and a great **heart**. I know because you've passed my tests and given your last drop of water to a dying plant. Here is the second charm. But you must promise to defend it from all enemies, especially the **Wizard of the Black Pearl**!"

"Thank you," I said, slipping the charm onto the

THE CLASPING HANDS
The Second Charm

Guarded in the Desert of Eyes and Ears by Tessa the Timeless Tortoise, also known as the Wise Shelled One and She Who Is Never in One Place, the Clasping Hands is a symbol of friendship. In the Kingdom of Fantasy, everyone is bound to offer help to whoever carries this charm and says the secret words: "We are friends!" As a symbol of friendship, this charm is also a kind of passport, and whoever wears it may cross any territory.

chain with the first one. *Two down, five to go,* I thought.

As if she were reading my thoughts, the tortoise said, "You will find the next charm in **RAINBOW VALLEY**."

Rainbow Valley

THE SEARCH FOR THE MEDALLION OF THE SUN AND THE MOON

Rainbow Valley

FLUTTERCOW, THE BUTTERFLY-COW

We took off for **RAINBOW VALLEY**. I was feeling good. We already had **two** of the seven charms, and we were going to a place called **RAINBOW VALLEY**. How bad could it be?

Still, after many hours, Chatterclaws began to complain. "My claws are *killing* me! If we have to walk much more I'm going to turn into a real crab!"

"Maybe we can call Blossom on the Chatterphone and she can send some kind of **FAIRY** transportation," I said.

The crab snorted, "There aren't any dragons or unicorns here!"

Then suddenly he cried, "I've got it! We can take a **FLYING COW**!"

No dragons
or unicorns?

"You're joking," I squeaked. "Cows don't fly!"

"Tell that to the one right behind you!" The crab chuckled.

I turned around, ready to call the crab's bluff, and let out a SHRIEK of surprise. Behind me I saw the strangest sight . . . yep, that's right, a **flying cow**!

The cow was the size of an ordinary cow, with horns, hooves, and a tail. But the rest of her was anything but ordinary. Her coat was white and dotted with sparkling, colorful spots. Around her neck was a chain of pink flowers. And on her back were giant, SHIMMERING butterfly wings!

"She's perfect!" Chatterclaws shouted. "Hold on. I think I'll catch her with my *lasso*!"

But as soon as the strange creature realized the crab was planning to catch her, she made a face at us and **fluttered** off.

Then I had an idea. I pulled out the second charm and held it up to the cow. I said the secret words, "**WE ARE FRIENDS!**"

Instantly, the cow's eyes widened. "Well, **moooove** on over, friends! I'm coming in for a landing!" she sang.

Light as the **breeze**, the cow landed on the ground.

Pfffft!

Hey, come back!

Meanwhile, Chatterclaws produced a book from his shell entitled *Creatures of the Kingdom of Fantasy from A to Z and Beyond.*

He paged through it quickly, then read aloud, "You must be Fluttercow, a butterfly-cow."

"That's me!" Fluttercow mooed. "At your service! Where are you headed?"

As Fluttercow helped us climb onto her back, Chatterclaws consulted our map. "We need to get the whatchamacallit . . . the **Medallion of the Sun and the Moon**, that's found in Rainbow —"

But before the crab could even finish his sentence, Fluttercow took flight, heading straight for the clouds!

Moldy mozzarella! That cow

was as **fast** as a jet liner!

I gripped on to a horn for dear life.

The cow continued to climb, until we were right in the middle of a **CLOUD**. Then she slowed down so we could admire the **moon** and the **stars** that filled the sky.

Of course, I had to open my eyes first, which were **SQUEEZED** shut in fear. But once I did, I discovered that the night sky is a beautiful sight!

During the flight Fluttercow told us all about how she turned from an ordinary cow into a **BUTTERFLY-COW** . . .

The Story of Fluttercow, the Butterfly-Cow

It all began a long time ago, on a beautiful, sunny day. There was a breeze waving through the grassy fields. I had just finished munching on some clover and was admiring the butterflies fluttering around me. Oh, how I wished I could be as nimble as them! And how I'd love to be able to fly! The butterflies were colorful, delicate, and as light as a feather. I, on the other hoof, was only black and white, and feeling like a big, huge—well, cow. Just then I heard someone shouting, "Help!"

I looked around but didn't see anyone.

I was about to lie down on the grass, but again I heard a shout. "Who can help the Queen of the Butterflies?"

I turned and finally saw a butterfly caught in the middle of a large spiderweb.

The butterfly had large, shimmering gold wings and a crown on her head made of tiny dewdrops.

I knew right away I had to help. With the bat of a hoof, I destroyed the web and freed the butterfly.

Once free, the butterfly queen flew up to me and asked, "What can I do for you, generous creature? You saved my life!"

I thought for a minute, and then I said, "Well, please don't think I'm crazy, but my greatest wish is to be able to fly."

The queen smiled. "Your wish is my command," she said. Then she brushed my shoulders with her wings, causing some of her golden shimmer to fall on me. Suddenly, from out of my back, two gorgeous, colorful wings sprouted! My coat became multicolored, and a chain of pink flowers appeared around my neck.

"From now on you will be called Fluttercow, the butterfly-cow!" said the queen. "You are a special cow. You can fly, and your milk will have a thousand different flavors. And when you eat the flowers of this necklace, you will gain extraordinary powers that will make you invincible!"

Since then, I have fluttered happily above the fields of the Kingdom of Fantasy.

GIVE UP YOUR PASSENGERS!

We flew on through the night. Then at **dawn** the cow announced, "Get ready—we've almost reached the **Colorful Forest**!"

I was congratulating myself on managing to **ReLaX** throughout the flight when it happened . . .

There are seven of us . . .

. . . we are cruel . . .

. . . we are evil . . .

Out of the clouds came seven **ENORMOUSE** vultures as black as night. They had **pink** heads; long, hooked beaks; and **SHARP TALONS**, and they wore evil expressions.

"A message for you, Fluttercow, from the **Wizard of the Black Pearl**," they squawked. "Give up your passengers, or you'll be sorry!"

I let out a terrified squeak and Chatterclaws's

. . . we have hooked beaks . . .

. . . and sharp talons . . .

. . . and we work for the Wizard of the Black Pearl!

shell turned **blue** with fear. But Fluttercow just laughed and said, *"HOW UDDERLY RIDICULOUS!* I will not give up my passengers! Fly away, featherheads!"

Now the vultures looked even more infuriated. What was Fluttercow doing? How could one butterfly-cow battle seven **sinister** vultures?

Then before I knew what was happening, she turned and yelled, "Hold on tight!"

Fluttercow bit one of the **FLOWERS** from her necklace. Suddenly, her horns started to spin and her wings beat so fast they became invisible! Then she began lashing out with sharp kicks that made her hooves **SPARKLE**.

The **vultures** fought back, but Fluttercow was like a **whirling** ninja cow warrior with wings! Who would have guessed a cow could have such amazing acrobatic moves?

When the last vulture flew away, I wanted to

cheer. Too bad I was GREEN with motion sickness!

Chatterclaws STUMBLED out of his shell, his eyes crossed from fear. "Oh, why did I choose this career? To think that I could be at the bottom of the SEA munching seaweed right now . . ." he muttered to no one in particular.

Then he shook himself and, clearing his throat, announced, "In the name of Blossom, the Queen of the Kingdom of Fantasy, I, Chatterclaws of the Seven Seas, her whatchamacallit—er, trusted messenger—congratulate you on this great victory over the—um, you know—Wizard of the Black Pearl's spies!"

He had barely finished his sentence when Fluttercow plunged headlong toward the ground, MOOING, "Get ready for landing!"

By the time we landed, my head was spinning and I was as GREEN as a pickle! Instead of

climbing off the cow like a noble knight, I slumped
to the ground, snoutfirst.

OH, HOW EMBARRASSING!

Meanwhile Chatterclaws leaped off the cow and
kissed the ground. "**I'm alive! I'm alive!**"
he cried. "Holy **sea stars**, I need a raise! This
job is getting more dangerous every day!"

Mooo!

Ugh!

I'm alive!

Smack!
Smack!

Hot Chocolate or a Milkshake?

I was feeling like my old self again when Fluttercow announced, "We've landed just in time for **breakfast**! What do you prefer: hot chocolate, a cappuccino, a **smoothie**, or a milkshake? What flavor?"

At first I was thinking maybe the butterfly-cow might have been **smacked** in the head during her battle with the vultures and wasn't thinking CLEARLY, but then I remembered something. Fluttercow had the power to make all kinds of **FLAVORED** milk beverages!

Once we had decided on drinks, Chatterclaws DISAPPEARED into his shell, returning with some **cheesy** Danish. What a feast!

I was enjoying my breakfast so much I completely

forgot we were on a **dangerous** mission. When I was done eating I sighed happily and began thinking about what I would have for lunch. A **strawberry** smoothie? A **CHOCOLATE** milkshake?

The possibilities were **endless**!

A second later Fluttercow brought me back to reality. "Time to get **MOOOVING**!" she advised, and soon we were soaring back into the sky.

Luckily, we were not attacked by evil vultures this time. Instead, we flew through a GRAY cloud and landed in a foggy GRAY valley.

We began walking on a GRAY path that led to a GRAY forest with GRAY apple trees.

Eventually, we ended up in

Wh-where are we?

Welcome, strangers!

a GRAY village with **bizarre** houses shaped like apples. All around us it sounded like a thousand voices were weeping. **How strange!**

Then someone approached us. It was a **gnome** who was—you guessed it!—completely GRAY!

The gnome wore a GRAY apple-shaped hat on his head, GRAY pants, GRAY boots, and, well, you get the point . . . he was GRAY.

Waaah! Sniff! Sniff!

With a sad voice, he said, "Welcome, strangers, to **RAINBOW VALLEY**! I, Firebeard, Leader of the Red-nosed Gnomes, welcome you."

I coughed. I mean, I didn't want to insult the gnome by pointing out the obvious, but what can I say? I'm a curious rodent. So I said, "We are honored to meet you, **Firebeard**. But . . . why is this place called **RAINBOW VALLEY** if everything around us is GRAY?"

Before I could even finish, the gnome began to weep, **BLOWING** his nose on my cape. "Ah, travelers who have come from far away . . . if you only knew! **Sob!**"

I felt awful. First, because I had made the gnome cry. And second, because he was making a **disgusting** mess of my cape! Yuck!

While **Firebeard** composed himself, Chatterclaws pulled out the book on the Kingdom of Fantasy and read aloud the page on

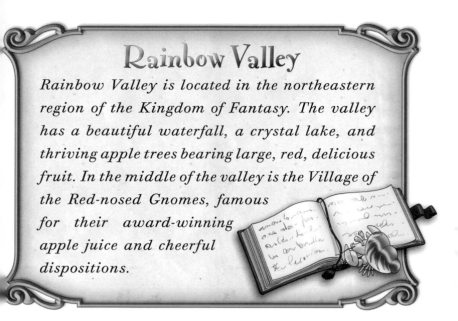

Rainbow Valley

Rainbow Valley is located in the northeastern region of the Kingdom of Fantasy. The valley has a beautiful waterfall, a crystal lake, and thriving apple trees bearing large, red, delicious fruit. In the middle of the valley is the Village of the Red-nosed Gnomes, famous for their award-winning apple juice and cheerful dispositions.

RAINBOW VALLEY. Apparently the place used to be filled with **COLOR**.

"Yes, our village was *bright* and beautiful." Firebeard nodded, once he had calmed down. "But one sad day, the **Wizard of the Black Pearl** flew over our land and demanded I hand over the enchanted charm given to me by Blossom."

The gnome wiped away another tear as he continued the story. "Of course I refused to give

up the charm, and the wizard flew into a rage. He proclaimed that he would punish our entire village by taking away our **happiness**.

"Before we knew what was happening, he used the **black pearl** around his neck to suck the **COLOR** out of everything around us . . . the houses, the fields, and even our clothes and skin! Since

then we've tried many times to make the apple juice we're famous for, but because the apples are GRAY, the juice is, well, not exactly JUICY, if you know what I mean."

I felt a PANG of sympathy for the gnomes. Bad apple juice for these gnomes would be like making bad cheese for us rodents. What a nightmare!

Firebeard dried his tears once again and finished sadly, "So we have **no** more colors, **no** more apple juice, and **no** more happiness in our village. If only the **PIXIE PAINTERS** would help us . . ."

I blinked. "Who are they?" I said.

apple apple

ALL FOR US, AND NONE FOR YOU!

Firebeard let out a long sigh and pointed to a spot in the distance where, behind the hills encircling the valley, a beautiful rainbow **shone**.

"Do you see those hills? There, at the end of the rainbow, the **SEVEN PIXIE PAINTERS** live. They possess the secret of **COLOR**, which they've guarded for centuries. When the wizard stole our colors, we asked the pixies for help, but they refused."

"How **terrible**!" I squeaked.

"How *rude*!" shouted the crab.

"How udderly unbelievable and selfish!" declared Fluttercow.

Then I told the gnome, "I'll convince the Pixie Painters to share!"

At this, Firebeard began to CRY again, blowing his nose loudly in my cape. Honk! "But you'll never do it! Those pixies are too stubborn!" he wailed.

I cut him off. "It's worth a try," I said. I wasn't sure I could convince the pixies to share, but I was sure of one thing: I needed to get my cape to the cleaner's. It was a mess!

It's hopeless . . .

It's worth a try!

We flew through the night and reached the Pixie Valley at dawn. Hiding behind a rock, we spied

seven pixies *DANCING* and **Singing**:

"We are the Pixie Painters!
We are never sad or blue,
for we own the rainbow colors:
They're all for us, and none for you!"

"Can you believe these guys?" Chatterclaws whispered. "I mean, would it really kill them to share their **COLORS**? I'm going to scuttle over there and give them each a good hard PINCH!"

I had to agree with the crab. These pixies needed to be taught a lesson in sharing. Still, something told me **PINCHING** them wasn't really the answer, so I said, "Hold on. I think we need to use our **BRAINS** to convince them."

The pixies had each grabbed a paintbrush and started painting. But instead of **enjoying** their individual colors, they **argued** with one another.

One pixie bragged, "I am **BLUE** like the sea. You wish you could be me!"

Another, the *yellow* pixie, snickered. "I am yellow like the sun. Your color is no fun!"

Then the **RED** pixie said to the *GREEN* pixie, "That green makes me sick! You look like a pickle! Ick!"

Soon enough, paint began flying all over the place.

We watched in fascination as blobs of **red**, orange, YELLOW, green, **BLUE**, **INDIGO**, and **ViOLet** soared through the air. Talk about a colorful argument!

Violet is pretty like a flower.
Your color is totally sour!

Indigo is the best.
Better than all the rest!

Hee, hee, hee!

ALLOW ME TO INTRODUCE MYSELF

After watching the Pixie Painters, it was pretty clear they wouldn't be winning any **kindness** awards. So how would we get through to a mean pack of PIXIES?

Right then Chatterclaws muttered, "I've got an idea."

He scuttled into his shell and came out with an artist's beret on his head, a **magnifying glass** in his left claw, and a painter's palette in his right. He strode out from behind the rock, examining the **RAINBOW** with his magnifying glass. "Oh, good day to you, kind pixies!" he said in a strange accent. "This **rainbow** is lovely! Is it your work?"

Hmmm . . .

Immediately, the pixies stopped arguing and boasted, "As certainly as sunshine follows rain, it's our rainbow!"

The crab handed them a business card and said, "Allow me to introduce myself. I am **MASTER CLAWS OF THE SEVEN COLORS**, Rainbow Expert! I am traveling through the Kingdom of Fantasy on a mission to find the Most Beautiful Rainbow Ever Known, to **AWARD** it with a special certificate signed by Queen Blossom."

> MASTER CLAWS
> OF THE SEVEN COLORS
> RAINBOW EXPERT

They were **shocked**. "We didn't know there were any **RAINBOW EXPERTS**..."

"Yes, well, I am an expert, all right. As **EXPERT** as they come. I know everything about whatchamacallits, I mean, *colors*.

Yep, that's me—just ask my assistant," the crab babbled.

Then he **PINCHED** me on the tail and I let out a *YELP*, causing the pixies to double over in laughter.

Encouraged by their laughter, Chatterclaws said, "Actually, I was wondering, **dear friends**, if you might do me a favor. You see, I seem to be a bit short on paint, and I was hoping you **KIND** pixies could **loan** me some of your colors." He held out his empty palette for the pixies to see.

No way! Our colors stay!

But the seven pixies all screamed, "We do not give our **colors** away! They're ours alone. Right here they'll stay!"

Thinking fast, I said, "So tell us, talented **PIXIE PAINTERS**, how do you get your colors?"

The **RED** pixie stepped forward and said,

paintbrush paintbrush paintbrush paintbrush paintbrush paintbrush paintbrush paintbrush paintbrush paintbrush paintbrush paintbrush paintbrush paintbrush

"Our colors come from our emotions, not from fancy magical potions." With the paintbrush in his hand, he painted part of a RAINBOW. The paint just appeared on the brush, like magic!

Suddenly, an idea came to me. First, I needed to tell the pixies a very sad story. The **saddest** story I could think of!

So I began, "Long ago, in a faraway land, lived a beautiful princess with **BLACK** hair, TURQUOISE eyes, and skin as WHITE as ivory. She wore a PINK silk gown covered with GREEN emeralds and RED rubies. In her palace garden, thousands of colorful flowers grew."

"Ohhh, how beautiful! How amazing!" the

pixies all murmured dreamily.

I continued, "One terrible day, an evil witch, **JEALOUS** of the princess's beauty, decided to steal all her colors. She snuck into the princess's palace in the middle of the night and took every single color . . ."

Waah! Your story has moved us to tears!

"Oh, how horrible!" **wailed** the pixies, beginning to cry.

The pixies' tears were as **colorful** as the rainbow. It was exactly what I was hoping for! Tears of red, orange, yellow, green, blue, indigo, and violet spilled onto the grass. Now all we had to do was capture the colors. But how? If only I had thought of this little problem before the pixies started **bawling** ...

I was about to start crying myself when the crab jumped to his claws. He gave me a wink, then quickly ran from one pixie to the next, gathering all of the **colors** on his palette.

As soon as Chatterclaws had collected the **tears**, we ran back to Fluttercow.

"Hey, where's our award for the Most Beautiful Rainbow Ever Known?"

the pixies shouted before we left.

That's when Chatterclaws tossed them a certificate. It read, "AWARD FOR THE STINGIEST PIXIES IN THE KINGDOM OF FANTASY!"

AWARD FOR THE STINGIEST PIXIES IN THE KINGDOM OF FANTASY

LET'S GET
TO WORK!

When we returned to the village, the gnomes cheered. Nothing like all the colors of the rainbow to brighten a GRAY day!

Still, before we painted the whole place, we decided to do a test. Chatterclaws painted all of the apples on one tree RED. Then Firebeard took them to the Apple Juice Factory.

1 basket of apples = 1 bottle of apple juice

The apples were **pressed** and **SQUASHED** to make juice. The resulting liquid was as golden as honey, perfectly **SWEET**, and smelled better than I ever could have imagined.

I mean, I still love my mozzarella milkshakes better than any other beverage, but this apple juice was **WHiSKER-LiCKiNG GOOD**! Now I understood why it was once the most famouse in all the Kingdom of Fantasy!

We **toasted** to the inhabitants of Rainbow Valley, then Chatterclaws cried, "Okay, enough celebrating! Let's get to work!"

We grabbed paintbrushes and began adding **COLOR** to everything: red roofs, green plants, yellow daisies, blue streams . . .

Finally, everything had its color back!

A little yellow here!

Hooray for color!

n-oh . . .

Answer: 19 apples

Firebeard grinned from ear to ear. It felt great to see the gnome smiling. Plus, it felt even better not to have him crying and **BLOWING** his nose in my cape! Ugh! I shuddered, remembering.

Anyway, where was I? Oh, yes. Firebeard was smiling away, and then he asked us, "How can we ever thank you, friends?"

I showed him the RING with Blossom's seal and quickly explained about our mission to collect the **seven enchanted charms**. We were hoping the gnome would give us the **third charm** to add to the golden chain.

"Of course," the gnome agreed. "You have proven I can trust you."

He rummaged in his coat and pulled out the **MEDALLION OF THE SUN AND THE MOON**, a golden charm enameled in **bright** colors, showing the sun and the moon entwined.

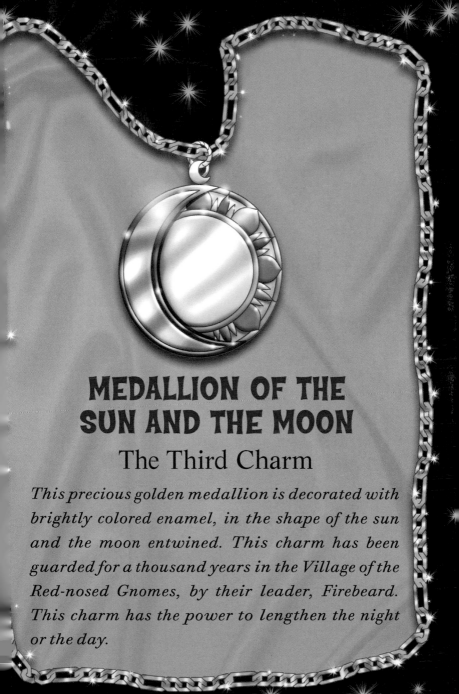

MEDALLION OF THE SUN AND THE MOON
The Third Charm

This precious golden medallion is decorated with brightly colored enamel, in the shape of the sun and the moon entwined. This charm has been guarded for a thousand years in the Village of the Red-nosed Gnomes, by their leader, Firebeard. This charm has the power to lengthen the night or the day.

WHAT KIND OF
COFFIN WOULD
YOU LIKE?

I strung the medallion on the chain along with
the other charms. Then the gnomes gave
us a boxful of—what else?—bottles of
apple juice!

Finally, it was time to leave, but
Fluttercow pulled me aside. "Sir Knight,
would you mind if I stayed here?" she
whispered. "This place is so **mooooving**!
It's extra colorful, just like me!"

What could I say? Of course, I agreed. "We'll
miss you," I told the butterfly-cow. "But thank you
for all your help. And don't worry about me. I'll
still have Chatterclaws."

Aunt Sandyclaws?

Just then the Chatterphone **RANG**, and the crab rushed to pick up.

"Hello, this is Chatterclaws . . . Aunt Sandyclaws, is that you? How are the crablings? What? You're in danger? Why? The Wizard of the Black Pearl? He's **draining** Scorpion Fish Bay? But that's where we live! Huh? The wizard wants **revenge** because I'm helping the knight? Of course . . . Don't worry . . . I'll be right there, crab's honor!"

Chatterclaws hung up looking **frantic**. "I'm so sorry, Sir Knight, Aunt Whatsit—I mean, the

We're in trouble!

whatchamacallit—I mean, there's not a moment to lose!"

Have you ever tried to talk to a **stressed-out** crab? Let me just say, it's not easy. Chatterclaws's pincers were *flying* all over the place! It was downright dangerous!

Eventually, he managed to calm down enough to explain the situation. It seemed that the **Wizard of the Black Pearl** had built a dam and was draining the bay where Chatterclaws's family lived.

"I must go immediately to Aunt Sandyclaws and her 113 **crablings**. I'll rejoin you when I can," the crab finished.

I told Chatterclaws not to worry—family should always come first. And even though I was **dying** to ask how Aunt Sandyclaws kept track of 113 **crablings**, it didn't seem like the right time.

Still, I did have one question: "How do I get to the **Towering Peaks**?" I asked.

"I'll tell you," Firebeard offered. "The Towering Peaks are the HIGHEST mountains in the Kingdom of Fantasy. The guardian of the fourth **CHARM** is the only one who lives there. His name is **Blizzard**, and he's a

ferocious white wolf lives there!

D-d-does he like mice?

FEROCIOUS white wolf, who loves fresh meat . . ."

"You mean like m-m-mouse meat?" I stammered.

Chatterclaws interrupted. "I hate to tell you, Knight, but he *loves* it! In fact, it's said that the wolf has been waiting centuries for one particular mouse. Hey, maybe that's *you*! Better be careful, or you might be his breakfast, or lunch, or dinner, or snack, or —"

"Thanks, I get it," I choked. "Any *life-saving* advice for me?"

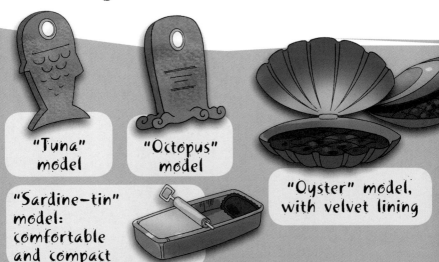

"Tuna" model

"Octopus" model

"Sardine-tin" model: comfortable and compact

"Oyster" model, with velvet lining

The crab sighed. "Let's see. You're going to a deserted place, where the only inhabitant is a **FEROCIOUS** wolf who loves mouse meat . . . hmm, I'd say, ɢᴏᴏᴅ ʟᴜᴄᴋ!"

Then he added, "But I have a cousin who owns a funeral home, and I'll make sure he takes care of you if you lose your fur on the **Towering Peaks**. What kind of coffin do you want? Do you prefer the **oyster** model, lined with **RED VELVET**, or the sardine-tin model? And for your headstone, do you want one shaped like a tuna or like an octopus?"

By this time I was ꜱʜᴀᴋɪɴɢ so hard I couldn't squeak.

"Don't worry," the crab continued. "All will go well . . . maybe. You'll probably survive, and we'll see each other soon . . . well, who knows. In any case, break a leg."

I squealed, "Break a leg?"

After I said good-bye to everyone, I took off. I thought I heard the crab shout something about watching out for the **White Spies**, but I wasn't really listening. No, I was too busy feeling **sorry** for myself.

RATS! I was missing my new friends already, and I had taken only a few steps!

Sigh . . .

The Realm of the Towering Peaks

THE SEARCH FOR THE DIAMOND STAR

The Realm of the Towering Peaks

WE ARE THE WHITE SPIES!

I walked for days and days as my heart grew heavier and heavier. I was **lonesome** for my friend Chatterclaws. I admit it—I missed his chattering, and even his **PINCHES**!

Finally, I reached the steep, icy path that led to the base of the Towering Peaks.

The climb was very difficult. I slipped on the ice with each step, while the howling wind pushed me around this way and that as if I were a yarn doll.

I was glad that the Red-nosed Gnomes had given me that apple juice along with some snack bars to keep up my strength.

When I reached the middle of my climb, I heard tiny voices shouting, "We are the White

SPIES, sent by the Wizard of the Black Pearl! How dare you climb our mountain!"

Then I heard a wicked **CACKLE** and saw what looked like an avalanche of snow crashing toward me! It was made of thousands of snowballs with **EVIL** little eyes.

I barely had time to yell, "**Heeeelp!**"

But there was **NO ONE** to help me.

Heeeelp!

Within minutes I was overcome by the snow **hurtling** down the mountain. I ended up completely buried in snow. Frozen feta! Would I ever escape from this prison of snow? I couldn't even tell which way was UP and which was down!

I tried to make some space, digging out a nook to move around in. Still, time was running out. I needed air! I was so scared, tears began to roll down my forehead . . . **drip! drip! drip!**

Wait . . . **DOWN** my forehead? It was then that I realized that I was stuck in the snow upside down! Now I knew which DIRECTION I needed to dig!

I flipped over and started to dig as quickly as possible, but it wasn't easy. My paws were FREEZING, and my teeth were chattering. **BRRRR!**

Oh, how I wished there was a way to **WARM UP**!

If Chatterclaws were with me, he would have invited me into the Chatterhouse and made me a nice cup of **HOT CHEESE**!

Or he would have had a *SHOVEL* to dig with . . .

I began to feel sleepy. Could I catch a tiny little **ratnap**? "**NO!**" a voice inside me screamed. "If you sleep, you'll end up a **FROZEN** mousicle!"

With a final burst of energy, I dug until, at last, I burst from the snow.

"**I did it!**" I squeaked.

I wish I could say I celebrated with a delicious **four-cheese** pizza, but instead disaster struck. First, I heard

Ooof!

an evil **cackle**. Then an enormouse piece of ice struck me on the head. Then I *fell* off a cliff!

I saved myself by **HANGING** on to the edge of the cliff by only my pawnail.

Squeeeak!

The next thing that happened was totally UNBELIEVABLE. Somehow I managed to pull myself up to safety! Don't ask me how I did it. Maybe I was so afraid of becoming a **scrambled** mouse I gained **HEROMOUSE** strength!

Aaaaah! I don't want to become scrambled mouse!

NICE WOLFY . . .

I continued my journey with **trembling** paws, following the icy path that glittered in the moonlight.

The wind continued to slow me down and **freeze** my whiskers and my tail. After one last difficult step, I found myself at the top of an icy peak.

I sat down to catch my breath, when suddenly a large, dark shape with four legs, small ears, and two GOLDEN eyes appeared before me.

I gnawed my whiskers in fear. Something told me it wasn't one of Santa Paws's reindeer welcoming me to the neighborhood.

A minute later the shape began to growl.

GRRRRRRRRRRRRRRRR . .

I wanted to run, but my paws were frozen to the spot!

Then the **creature** took a step forward and I saw that it was an enormouse wolf with pure **white** fur.

Heeelp!

Suddenly, I understood. This had to be **Blizzard**, the white wolf. Well, I certainly could see where he got his name. His white fur blended right into the snow.

I looked around to see if there was any escape, and that's when I spotted another horrifying sight. Piles and piles of **BONES**!

Holey cheddar chunks! What if these were the skeletons of all the adventurers who came before me looking for the fourth enchanted charm?

I looked up to find the wolf staring at me like I was a **juicy** steak at Cinderfur's Sizzling Steakhouse. He gnashed his sharp teeth.

Right then I remembered the crab's words: "He's been waiting centuries for a particular mouse . . ."

Was it true? Was I that mouse?

The wolf took a step forward, still growling, ears laid back, fur **standing** on end, looking ready to attack!

"Nice wolfy . . ." I squeaked.

Suddenly, I noticed something. The wolf's right
PAW was bleeding, leaving prints in the snow. It
must have been *hurt*, because he was placing it
gingerly on the ground. Then I saw that there was
a large *thorn* in it!

Forgetting that he was probably about to eat me,
I said, "Would you like me to pull that *thorn*
out?"

The wolf's eyes narrowed **suspiciously**, as if trying to figure out my real intentions.

I took a step forward, paws open wide, to show that I wasn't armed and that I came in **peace**. Then I took his paw and delicately started to take out the thorn.

The paw was swollen, and it must have hurt a lot, because the wolf growled loudly. But with one firm tug I pulled out the **thorn** and showed it to him. "See? This thorn was hurting you, but now it's all over," I told him. "Your paw will heal quickly!"

I poured **WATER** from my canteen over the wound to clean it, and spread some medicinal **HERB** salve that Firebeard had given me on it. Finally, I ripped a strip of seaweed from my cape and carefully used it to bandage his paw.

I must say, the wolf was an **EXCELLENT**

patient. And when I finished tending to him, he thanked me with a ꬒlᴜrpy lick!

I knew then that his **FEROCIOUS** teeth gnashing was just an act!

Lick, lick!

Hee, hee, hee!

Go Now!

Even though the wolf was now my friend, I still had a problem. I had to find the fourth CHARM.

I stood waiting for a sign, a signal, a text message . . .

As if in response to my THOUGHTS, the white wolf turned to the moon and howled. I raised my snout, and in the dark sky I saw millions of stars!

Awoooooooo!

All of a sudden, one star shone **BRiGHTER** than the others.

Then I heard a voice say, "That star is the **FOURTH CHARM**. You must go and capture it."

I looked around, **confused**, because there was no one else there — only the wolf.

The voice repeated, "Go now. Quickly!"

It was then that I realized it was the *white wolf* who was speaking! But his voice had been only in my head. *How can I get that star?* I thought.

"Don't worry, I'll help you," I heard in my head.

I grinned. He could hear my thoughts! I wondered if I could learn how to read minds when I got back home. Sometimes   can be soooo overrated.

I was still thinking about reading minds when

the wolf took a deep breath and **blew** hard into the freezing night air.

Like *magic*, his breath froze into a shining  **i c e** bridge, which led all the way up to the star! The wolf bowed so that I could jump on his back. Then he began to race along the *icy* bridge, up into the night sky.

I tried not to look at the   view.

Did I mention I'm afraid of heights? And of slipping on the ice, SPIDERS, snakes, elevators, and especially the dark? On all sides of the bridge was endless DARK.

How terrifying!

Still, I tried to be strong. After all, I remembered, in order to get the FOURTH CHARM I had to prove my courage.

After about a **BILLION** years racing along the icy bridge (well, okay, it wasn't quite that long), we finally reached the bright **SHINING** star. The wolf nudged me to reach for it, and so I did. The star was small and **SPARKLED** with the light of a thousand diamonds!

The star!

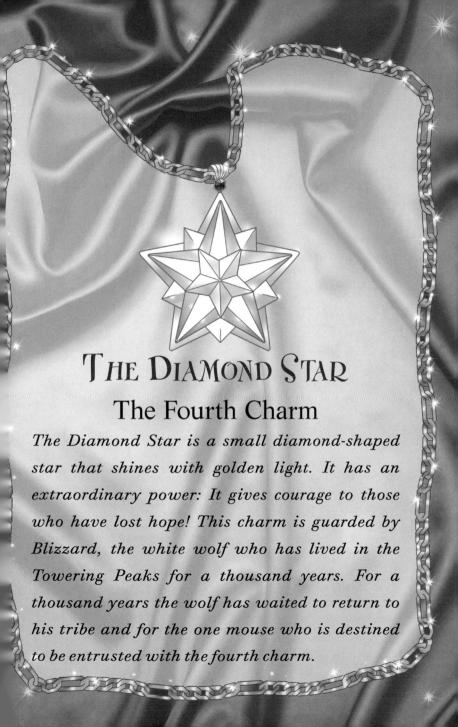

THE DIAMOND STAR
The Fourth Charm

The Diamond Star is a small diamond-shaped star that shines with golden light. It has an extraordinary power: It gives courage to those who have lost hope! This charm is guarded by Blizzard, the white wolf who has lived in the Towering Peaks for a thousand years. For a thousand years the wolf has waited to return to his tribe and for the one mouse who is destined to be entrusted with the fourth charm.

The wolf wagged his tail with satisfaction. Then I heard his voice in my head. "For a thousand years I've been the guardian of the **Diamond Star**, the fourth enchanted charm. And for a thousand years I've been waiting for one special mouse. A mouse who is strong, **brave**, and **COURAGEOUS**. Now that you have reached me, I can pass the precious Diamond Star on to you and finally return to my tribe, the tribe of the WHITE WOLVES."

My friend!

I grinned. Who would have guessed I, Geronimo Stilton, or, er, Sir Geronimo of Stilton, could be strong, **brave**, and COURAGEOUS! I puffed up my chest and suddenly felt a new sense of daring and confidence.

Unfortunately, the feeling didn't last long. A moment later the wolf explained the next part of my mission. "You must retrieve the **Crystal Feather** found on the Crystal Planet. Many heroes have tried to reach it, but no one has ever succeeded . . . or returned," he said.

As my whiskers trembled in fear, my mind filled with questions and worries. How would I get to the **CRYSTAL PLANET**? How would I find the Crystal Feather? Why couldn't these adventures take place somewhere fun, like a beach resort or **cheese factory**?

"Don't worry—I will help you," Blizzard

continued soothingly. Oops, I had forgotten he was reading my mind! How humiliating!

The next thing I knew I was sitting on the wolf's back. Then he LAUNCHED into a gallop across the icy bridge, until we were right next to a comet with a long, shining tail.

"Quickly, Sir Knight, grab hold of that comet. You can do it!" the wolf told me.

I was about to explain to the wolf about my fear of FLYING, but before I knew what was happening, he threw me toward the comet! What could I do? I grabbed on for dear life and shot off into the darkness. Oh, how do I get myself into these scary situations?

The comet flew at supersonic speeds through the starry sky. Each time it passed a meteorite, I let out a squeal of terror. Headlines flashed in my mind: *Stilton, Lost in Space!*; *Meteorite Melts Mouse!*

Eventually, though, the meteorites FADED away, and there were fewer stars. I started to feel peaceful in the silent sky. We continued on through the dark night until I saw a tiny planet SHINING up ahead, getting closer and closer . . .

THE CRYSTAL PLANET

THE SEARCH FOR THE CRYSTAL FEATHER

1. CRYSTAL MOUNTAINS
2. SEA OF A THOUSAND MIRRORS
3. THE OAK OF TRUTH
4. THE WAY OF THE PURE HEART
5. THE PATH OF FORGOTTEN HEROES
6. THE COMET'S LANDING PLACE
7. THE HILLS OF TRANSPARENCY
8. THE FOUNTAIN OF SINCERITY
9. THE GREAT STAR CLOCK

THE CRYSTAL PLANET

CLINK! CLINK! CLINK!

When the comet reached the planet, I understood why it shone so brightly. It was made entirely of **SPARKLING** crystal! The comet headed at top speed toward a locked, majestic **crystal** gate.

"Wait! I don't have a key!" I squeaked. But then, as if by MAGIC, the gate opened to let us pass. It seemed to be waiting for our arrival!

HOW STRANGE!

Even stranger, the comet suddenly turned into a maiden with _long_ golden hair. Her voice sounded like crystal glasses **clinking** as she started speaking.

> _"Traveler from far away, heed my advice:_
> _You must find the scale, a truth-telling device._
> _If you are sincere, then the fifth charm is for you._
> _If not, then beware—you'll turn into a statue!"_

Traveler from far away . . .

I gulped. I had no idea what the golden maiden was talking about. What was a truth-telling device? And where was I supposed to find it? Plus, what did she mean about turning into a STATUE? Oh, why did everyone always have to speak in riddles? It was enough to drive a mouse up a clock!

To make matters worse, before I could even ask the maiden one question, she transformed back into a comet and ZIPPED off into the sky.

"Come back!" I squeaked. But it was too late. The comet was gone, and I soon found myself all alone, LOST and afraid, on this mysterious planet. I was feeling so lonely I burst into sobs, but my tears clinked when they fell to the ground.

Clink! Clink! Clink! Clink!

Had I been transformed into a statue made of crystal? No—when I pinched myself, I still squeaked. **Holey cheese**, what a scare!

I shook myself. "There's no time to feel sorry for yourself!" I said aloud, trying to give myself a **pep talk**. "You've got to get that **fifth charm** to add to all of the other charms you've collected, so you can help Blossom."

Okay, I know it sounds a little weird that I was talking aloud to myself, but I had no choice. I couldn't exactly **WHIP** out my cell phone and call a friend. (For starters, I had forgotten to bring my phone and, even if I had, I doubt the connection would work way up in space.)

I walked along a **CRYSTAL** path through a valley with a **CRYSTAL** blue stream. Next to the stream were colorful **CRYSTAL** flowers, and on the horizon I spied shimmering **CRYSTAL** mountains.

Then I noticed a horrifying sight. Along the path stood crystal **STATUES**. There were knights, scholars, wizards, maidens, and more. Each wore a SURPRISED expression. I gulped. Cheese sticks! These were the heroes

D-d-don't mind m-m-m-me!

who had tried to win the Crystal Feather. They had been transformed into **CRYSTAL STATUES**!

CONGRATULATIONS! YOU'RE HONEST!

Just then I heard a **sweet** song. I looked around and saw a large **scale** made of gilded crystal, and a nightingale, who was singing:

"Stranger who hails from far away,
listen closely to what I say!
To prove your worth, you must pass this test,
so sit on the scale—please be my guest.
If your heart is sincere,
you'll have nothing to fear.
If you tell only lies,
it will be your demise!"

I **chewed** my whiskers in a panic. This time I understood the riddle. If I didn't pass the test, I'd be turned into a crystal statue!

SHAKING, I sat on one side of the scale.

Then the bird pulled a crystal feather from its tail, placed it on the other side of the scale, and began to **sing** again:

"A sincere heart is feathery light.
A heart that lies is heavy and tight."

Anxiously, I wracked my brain trying to remember if I had told any LIES. Well, there was that one time when I told my aunt Sweetfur that I liked the tie she had bought me for my birthday when I really didn't. But I just said that because I didn't want to **hurt** her feelings.

The sides of the scale started to move back and forth, **UP** and **down**, **UP** and **down**, **UP** and **down**!

I closed my eyes. Would I stay a mouse, or

would I be transformed into a **CRYSTAL STATUE**? I didn't even want to think about it!

When I opened my eyes I saw the scale had settled. It was perfectly **BALANCED**!

CHEESE NIBLETS! What a relief.

With a flourish, the bird presented the Crystal Feather to me, singing, "Congratulations—you

Just for you!

The Crystal Feather!

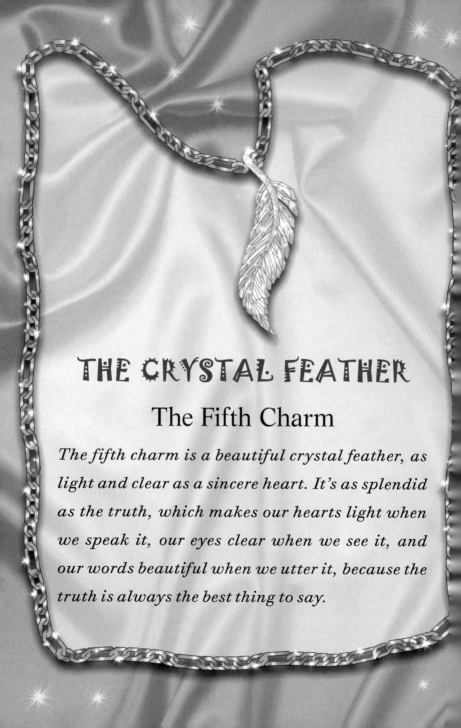

THE CRYSTAL FEATHER

The Fifth Charm

The fifth charm is a beautiful crystal feather, as light and clear as a sincere heart. It's as splendid as the truth, which makes our hearts light when we speak it, our eyes clear when we see it, and our words beautiful when we utter it, because the truth is always the best thing to say.

did it! You're honest; it's true! Now this special feather will belong to you!"

I *hurried* to attach the charm to the golden chain along with the other **FOUR CHARMS** I had already acquired on my journey. I was so relieved that I was not being turned into a statue, I practically **sang** with joy.

Ow!
It Burns!

I was so busy basking in my success I almost forgot I was on a **crystal** planet far off in the galaxy. Suddenly, it occurred to me I had no way to get off the planet!

Rat-munching rattlesnakes! Maybe I would end up lost in space after all!

Luckily, the nightingale came to my rescue. She told me to hurry back to the **LONG** path and find the **golden** maiden again. I could hitch a ride with her when she turned back into a comet.

I raced along the path, paws **FLYING**. Just in the nick of time I found the maiden, and we took off into the night.

Whew!

We zipped past stars and planets until I realized

the sky was growing **BRIGHTER** and the comet was growing paler. Oh, no!

I took out the Medallion of the Sun and the Moon and wished that the night would last longer. It worked! Soon, I saw the sea right below us.

Then I heard a voice call out, "**YOO-HOO! KNIGHT!**"

Help!

Yoo-hoo! Knight!

I'm falling!

It was Chatterclaws, on board a strange hot-air balloon! He waved his claw and I waved back, but just at that moment the star of the morning appeared. The sky grew bright, the comet disappeared, and . . . I fellllllll!

I thought I would fall into the sea, but just then I realized that there was a rock below me, with a large and mysterious castle on it.

I was headed right for the roof! Blistering blue cheese! I was about to become scrambled mouse casserole (bones included)!

Instead, though, I fell **STRAIGHT** down the palace chimney.

Have you ever looked in a chimney? They're usually **DARK** and filled with soot. This chimney was no exception. I coughed all the way down. Yuck!

I made a mental note to tell the castle owners they needed a chimney sweeper. Right away!

The good news is: Instead of falling onto a hard stone floor and smashing my poor **furry** body into

bits, I had fallen into the kitchen fireplace, right into a **POT** full of vegetable soup. All the **SOFT** pieces of vegetables broke my fall.

The bad news is: The soup had been on the fire, and it was **BURNING** hot! I jumped right out of

SPLASH!

It burns!

the pot, shouting, "**Ow! It burns!**"

As I was shouting, I discovered that there were **hot** peppers in the soup! I accidentally swallowed one, and tears sprang from my eyes as I cried, "**Ow! So spicy!**"

CRAB SOUP— CLAWS INCLUDED!

A moment later, someone else hurtled down the chimney, and, like me, fell into the pot of boiling soup.

"**Ow! It burns!**" the creature shrieked, jumping out of the pot, just as I did.

It was Chatterclaws, who got up, muttering, "*Sizzling seaweed!* I almost became crab soup—claws included!"

"I'm so glad you're here!" I told the crab. "Did you save your aunt and all the crablings?"

"Yes!" he replied. "I called a meeting of my whole family, and together we destroyed the dam that was draining Scorpion Fish Bay!"

Then he grew serious and murmured, "Now I need to tell you, Whatsyourface, you've fallen straight into the right thingamajig, where you'll find the next whatchamacallit . . ."

"I don't understand a word you're saying!" I protested.

He PINCHED me. "It's not your fault, Whatsyourname. You were probably BORN this way. I mean, you can't help it if you don't understand any thingamabobs . . ."

Finally, I squeaked, "Please stop! I need to find the place where the sixth charm is hidden!"

He shook his head. "That's what I've been trying to tell you! We're already here!"

My **eyes** widened. "Huh? Do you mean to say that this is the whatchamacallit—I mean, the right place?"

The crab sighed. "Must I spell **everything** out for you? The answer is yes! We're already here!" Chatterclaws exclaimed, disappearing into his shell.

At first I thought he had gone inside to take a nap. Was I that **annoying**? But a minute later he returned carrying *The Dictionary of the Kingdom of Fantasy* and showed me a picture of a place called **the Castle of Dreams**.

"So that's where I'll find the **Silver Unicorn**," I said.

"Yes, it's here," the crab agreed, lowering his voice. "But you'd better be careful. The Castle of Dreams isn't exactly dreamy. In fact, it's full of **traps**!"

The Castle of Dreams

THE SEARCH FOR THE SILVER UNICORN

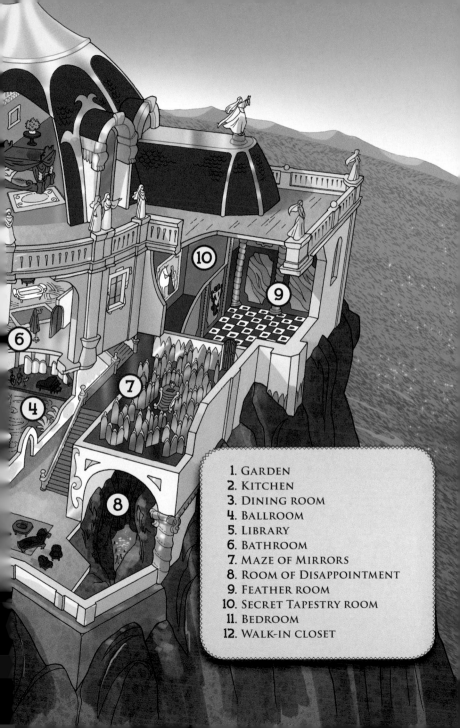

1. GARDEN
2. KITCHEN
3. DINING ROOM
4. BALLROOM
5. LIBRARY
6. BATHROOM
7. MAZE OF MIRRORS
8. ROOM OF DISAPPOINTMENT
9. FEATHER ROOM
10. SECRET TAPESTRY ROOM
11. BEDROOM
12. WALK-IN CLOSET

THE CASTLE OF DREAMS

Even though I was thrilled that we had fallen from the sky directly into the **Castle of Dreams**, our next destination (what were the chances of that?), I was worried.

For one thing, I always found castles a little scary. On the outside, they looked **MASSIVE** and **SPOOKY**. And on the inside, they had lots of secret corridors and high ceilings that made everything **echo** when you squeaked.

Squeak!

I tried to ask Chatterclaws about the **TRAPS**, but he just snorted. *Go on...* "What? You think I've got an instruction manual on the place?"

I sighed. I'd just have to keep my eyes open for anything suspicious.

I grabbed a GOLDEN candelabra, and, with the crab trailing after me, I began to explore the rooms of that *mysterious* castle.

I have to say, the castle was every mouse's dream. I guess that's where it got its name — the Castle of Dreams! The entranceway was bright CHEDDAR YELLOW, and there were bowls of cubed cheese all around. The kitchen was huge and had a MASSIVE refrigerator, an industrial-size stove, and a full pantry.

The dining table was set with a FEAST large enough to feed my family, my friends, my friends' friends, my neighbors, my neighbors' friends . . . Well, you get the idea. There was a TON of food!

There was a library with rare books; a

marble bathroom with a tub already full of warm, cheese-scented water; and a closet with all kinds of clothes in my size!

I must admit, I stayed for a while in the dining room. How could I resist? The food was so **tasty**!

Wow!

I had some mac and cheese, slices of **SWISS** on crackers, a pear and some Brie, and a piece of chocolate cheesecake.

Yum!

Then, satisfied, I visited the kitchen and made myself a nice mug of **CHAMOMILE** tea to help digest all that food. After waiting a few hours to digest, I took a nice warm bubble bath.

How relaxing!

Then I sat in the large **BALLROOM** on a comfy velvet chair. At the center of the room, an **invisible** orchestra was playing sweet music.

Finally, I **climbed** upstairs to the bedroom,

put on pajamas, got in bed, closed my eyes, and started to snore.

That's when I felt someone pinch my nose.

I woke up with a JUMP. "Ow!"

Chatterclaws was yelling in my ear, "Wake up! Have you completely forgotten about the search for the whatchamacallit—I mean, the ENCHANTED CHARM?"

The crab scoffed and continued, "If you haven't already figured it out, all these beautiful whatsits are just illusions, prepared by the **Wizard of the Black Pearl** to distract you from your search for the charm!"

I *rubbed* my eyes unhappily. Rats! I was having such a nice dream . . .

TURN RIGHT, NOW STRAIGHT, NOW LEFT . . .

I got out of bed, threw aside the pajamas, and said good-bye to the pillows. Oh, how I wished I could take those pillows with me. They were sooooo comfortable. Not too **plush**, not too hard. It was like sleeping on a *cloud*!

I started down the corridor with the crab followed me, **pinching** my tail now and then "to keep me awake." Ouch!

Eventually, we found ourselves entering an immense room. By the entrance, a sign said MAZE OF MiRRORS.

As soon as I looked around, I realized that the sign was a good description. It was a labyrinth full of mirrors!

The walls were made of **huge** mirrors, reflecting off each other so every image appeared thousands of times! Moldy mozzarella! I was getting **dizzy** just standing still!

Worried, I asked Chatterclaws, "How will we make it through the maze without getting lost?"

Tapping a claw to his forehead, he boasted, "Don't worry, Sir Knight, I found a map of the MAZE in *The Dictionary of the Kingdom of Fantasy.* I've got it all right here in my whatchamacallit — I mean, my BRAIN — turn by turn!"

That made me feel a little more confident. We entered the maze and continued along our way with Chatterclaws shouting out directions, "Turn **right**! Now straight! Now LEFT . . . now **right** . . . now straight . . . now LEFT . . ."

But after a while, disaster struck. Chatterclaws stopped shouting directions. He had **forgotten** them!

"Oops," he muttered.

I sat down and began to sob. How could this be happening to me? I was a GOOD MOUSE. I never caused any trouble. Well, there was that one time when I accidentally cut in front of an old lady mouse at the Shop and Nibble. She was so TINY, I didn't even see her!

Anyway, where was I? Oh, yes, I was **wailing** away about being lost forever, never finding the Silver Unicorn, never completing the mission and blah, blah, blah, when suddenly something STRANGE happened.

The Diamond Star that I wore around my neck began to shine, pointing the way out of the labyrinth!

The **LiGHt** led us to the center of the maze, where I discovered . . . the **Silver Unicorn**! Without thinking, I grabbed the charm.

"**IT COULD BE A TRICK!**" Chatterclaws tried to warn me.

But it was too late.

Suddenly, the floor opened beneath me and I fell into a trap set by the **Wizard of the Black Pearl**. And as I fell, I realized the charm wasn't even the real thing. How did I know? The unicorn's eyes weren't **blue**. They were **BLACK** pearls!

TRY NOT TO SNORE!

I fell into the trap with a loud **thud**! Above me, I saw the crab, shaking his head and waving a claw. "I told you so," he scolded.

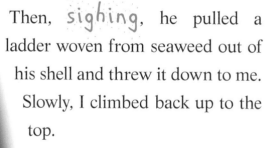

I told you so!

Then, *sighing*, he pulled a ladder woven from seaweed out of his shell and threw it down to me. Slowly, I climbed back up to the top.

After showing Chatterclaws the **FAKE** unicorn, we continued the search for the real charm. The **Diamond Star** showed us the way to go. Turn by turn, we left the winding **MAZE OF MIRRORS**.

We found ourselves in a large, ornate room with gold spiraled columns and a black-and-white marble floor. On each marble tile there was carved a COAT OF ARMS. It showed a shield divided in two, with a feather on one side and a unicorn on the other.

I stared at the floor, thinking. The picture of the UNICORN had to mean something . . . but what?

THE FAKE CHARM

"Well, what do we do now?" the crab asked, **TAPPING** his claw impatiently on the tile.

To tell the truth, I had no idea what to do next. But I didn't want Chatterclaws to get on my case, so I said, "I'm thinking."

I stared at the floor until the images SWAM before my eyes. What did they mean?

Just then I focused on something strange. On

the wall in front of me was a **STONE** plaque with the same **COAT OF ARMS** carved into the stone: the feather and the **UNICORN**. It was then that I realized the shape of the feather was *identical* to the fifth enchanted charm, the **Crystal Feather**!

It's the same . . .

ONE TILE IS DIFFERENT FROM THE REST. WHICH IS IT?

A secret passage!

Answer: It's the tile with the colors switched, at the top left, between the columns.

I grabbed the feather and placed it against the coat of arms. It fit perfectly into the carving! It seemed to be a key—the wall **SPRANG** open and started to rotate, revealing a **secret passage** that led to a hidden room!

In the room was a huge tapestry that showed a beautiful **GREEN** valley, a unicorn with a silver horn, and a young maiden. A crystal clear waterfall gushed in the background.

Written at the bottom of the tapestry were these words:

If you fall asleep right here,
your dreams will turn crystal clear!
So go to sleep and dream away,
and you will have a better day!

How marvelous!

If you fall asleep right here, your dreams will turn crystal clear!
So go to sleep and dream away, and you will have a better day!

THE POWER
OF DREAMS

Chatterclaws grinned. "It's your lucky day, What'syourname! You said you were sleepy, and now you need to dream in order to find the next charm!"

Then he *curled* up inside his seashell, yawning, "Sweet dreams. And try not to snore, okay?"

A moment later, he was the one **snoring**!

Luckily, I was so tired I fell asleep despite the snoring and began to **DReam** . . .

I dreamed that I was inside the tapestry! I heard the birds **chirping**, the leaves *rustling*, and the water in the brook **babbling**.

I followed a path that led to a clearing. A moment later, the maiden and the unicorn appeared. "We are the guardians of the sixth charm. Only those who know how to dream may receive this gift," they said in unison. "Your dreams are full of *goodness*, which is why you can understand us."

I was amazed. Who would guess I would find the CHARM in a dream, or that a unicorn and a maiden could speak so well in unison! How did they do that?

The maiden and the unicorn led me to the babbling brook. I couldn't believe it: At the bottom *shimmered* the **Silver Unicorn** charm!

But when I grabbed it, I felt myself **spin** in a vortex. Holey cheese! Was it another **trap**?

No. A second later, I woke up with the charm in my paw!

Now there was only one last charm left to find. Then my **MISSION** would be complete!

The Silver Unicorn
The Sixth Charm

The Silver Unicorn is a small silver charm shaped like a unicorn, with eyes made of two precious turquoise stones. It is guarded in a secret room inside the mysterious Castle of Dreams. This charm represents the importance of dreams. Only one who knows how to dream of beauty and goodness with their eyes closed and with their eyes open can change the world.

YOU HAVE A
SWIMSUIT, RIGHT?

I found myself back in the room with the **tapestry**, clutching the Silver Unicorn in my paws. I slid the charm onto the chain with the others, and we headed for the front door of the castle.

I was thinking the worst was over, but when we got outside, a **frightening** storm raged. Waves CRASHED against the rock, and terrifying flashes of **LIGHTNING** lit up the sky.

"Well, the only way back to land is to swim. You have a swimsuit, right?" Chatterclaws said in a strangely **calm** voice.

"Are you out of your shell?!" I squeaked. "There's no way I'm going swimming in the middle of a raging storm!"

Chatterclaws laughed. "Oh, don't be such a **drama mouse**, Whatsyourface!" he scoffed. "Just think, if you get hit by a *lightning bolt*, you'll have a really interesting story to tell . . . if you live. Plus, I have a relative who works in a hospital, so if we need to **REVIVE** you, he can help! But I can't guarantee you'll live."

I grabbed on to a **ROCK** and shouted, "No, I can't do it! I'm afraid of the ocean!"

Just then I heard a frightened voice shout, "Help!"

What a storm!

On the rock in front of me, there was a yellow fish with blue stripes *wriggling* in terror, gasping for breath.

Forgetting about the storm, I ran to him and tossed him back into the water.

As he swam through the **waves**, I heard him cry, "Thank you, kind Knight. You saved my life! If you ever need anything, you can count on **FINN**! That's me!"

I had just said good-bye to the **fish** when I saw an enormouse hurricane forming in the distance, leaving huge waves in its path.

At its center were two evil eyes—searching for us! A deep voice thundered, *"I WILL GET YOU!"*

Chatterclaws immediately burrowed into his shell for protection. That seashell sure came in handy. I mean, it wouldn't help you escape a

I will get you!

hurricane, but
you could at least
get comfortable
before **DISASTER**
struck. Maybe
even have some
cheese slices or a few
cheddar potato chips.

I was thinking about
chips when the
hurricane lifted
us up and carried
us away, ending up
holding us over a huge
WHIRLPOOL.

A second later, the
hurricane dropped
us down
into

the deep sea, into a **DARK** and terrifying cavern.

"I have b-b-bad news, Knight," Chatterclaws stammered, peeking out from his shell. "We're in the Mysterious Abyss!"

The Mysterious Abyss

THE SEARCH FOR THE GOLDEN PEARL

1. WHIRLPOOL GORGE
2. BLACK CORAL REEF
3. EMPTY SHELL DUMP
4. GREAT PEARL BANK
5. BOTTOMLESS ABYSS
6. PRISON OF DESPAIR
7. REFUGE OF LOST FISH
8. CAVE OF DEEPEST DARKNESS
9. CLIFF OF DREAMS OF FREEDOM

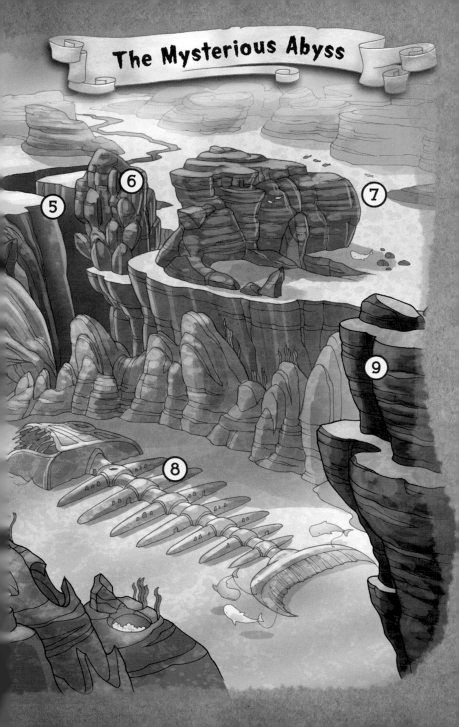

SQUISSSH! SWISSSH! SQUISSSH!

"Deep breaths," I told myself, practicing a stress-relieving technique I had learned from my old psychiatrist, **DR. SHRINKFUR**.

Unfortunately, the good doctor had never given me any tips on how to deal with a *monstrously* terrifying **GIANT SQUID**!

SQUISSSH!
SWISSSH!
SQUISSSH!

Let us go!

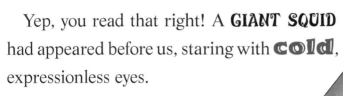

Yep, you read that right! A **GIANT SQUID**
had appeared before us, staring with **cold**,
expressionless eyes.

Chatterclaws just had time to shriek,
"It's been nice knowing you, Knight!"
before he fainted.

Then the squid grabbed us
with his long, **slimy** tentacle.
Aaaaah!

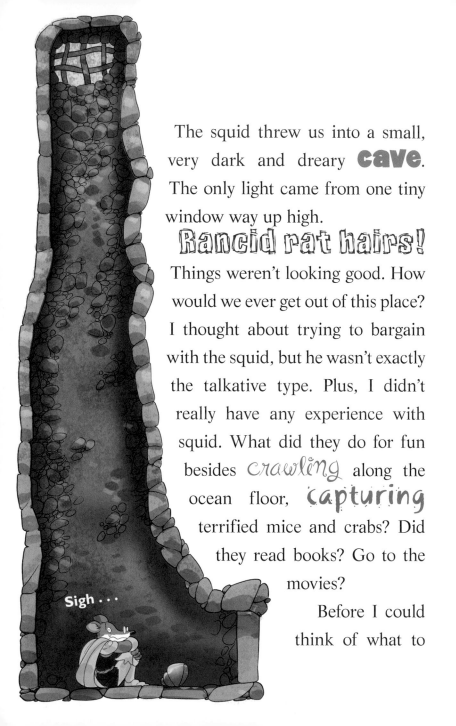

The squid threw us into a small, very dark and dreary **cave**. The only light came from one tiny window way up high.

Rancid rat hairs!

Things weren't looking good. How would we ever get out of this place? I thought about trying to bargain with the squid, but he wasn't exactly the talkative type. Plus, I didn't really have any experience with squid. What did they do for fun besides *crawling* along the ocean floor, *capturing* terrified mice and crabs? Did they read books? Go to the movies?

Before I could think of what to

Sigh . . .

say to him, the squid swam away.
SIGH . . .

Now I had no one to talk to.
Chatterclaws was still passed out in
his shell, and I was beginning to feel
like a total failure. The **darkness**
filled me with sadness.

Just when I was feeling like
all was lost, I spotted something
shining in my seaweed bag.
I placed a paw in the bag and
pulled out a little **stardust**.
It must have fallen in there when I
was traveling on the comet!

That **LIGHT** cheered me
up. Now I knew what I had
to do.

First I needed to
revive Chatterclaws,

Wow!

so I picked him up and **shook** him. "Wake up!" I squeaked. "I need your help!"

The crab crawled out of his shell, looking annoyed. "Smoking sardines! Did you have to *shake* so hard? You broke the chandelier in my dining room!" he complained.

After apologizing, I pointed to the **little** window above us and said, "Do you have something that could help us get out of that window?"

Chatterclaws disappeared back in his shell and reappeared with a rope with a *hook* on the end.

"Great!" I squeaked, getting excited.

I managed to snag the hook on the bars of the window, then I climbed up the rope. Pushing my nose through the bars I yelled, "*Help*!"

Suddenly, I spied Finn, the fish I had rescued!

"*I'll help you!* Be right back!" he cried, swimming off.

THE WIZARD OF
THE BLACK PEARL

As I waited in the prison, I thought about the seventh charm, the GOLDEN PEARL. Where would I find it?

Just then, an icy voice called out, "Did you really think you could escape me?!"

A **tentacle** opened the door to our prison and pulled us outside.

I was so scared I could hardly breathe. Or maybe that was just the tentacle squeezing the life out of me! **GULP!**

When we got outside we saw the squid holding up a

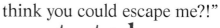

dark shell with someone sitting on it, as if on a throne. The dark figure wore a long purple robe and had a black pearl around his neck.

It didn't take a rocket scientist to figure out we had finally come face-to-face with the infamouse **Wizard of the Black Pearl**!

"So, you must be Sir Geronimo of Stilton, otherwise known as the Knight of the Seven Seas. You're looking for the GOLDEN PEARL, right?" the wizard sneered.

I coughed, hoping the wizard wouldn't notice I was shaking like a leaf. "I am here in the name of Queen Blossom, to ask the guardian of the Golden Pearl to give it to me!" I squeaked.

The wizard burst out with an evil laugh and replied, "Well, you've found what you're looking for. But I have a surprise for you: The guardian is Sid, the giant squid, but I've **hypnotized** him, and now he is my slave!"

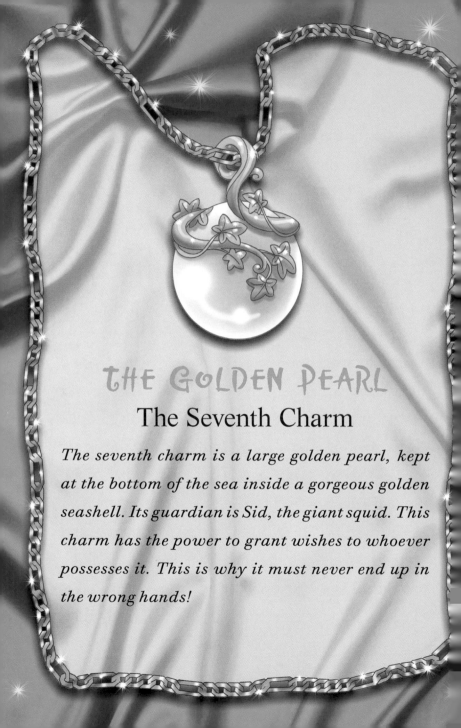

THE GOLDEN PEARL

The Seventh Charm

The seventh charm is a large golden pearl, kept at the bottom of the sea inside a gorgeous golden seashell. Its guardian is Sid, the giant squid. This charm has the power to grant wishes to whoever possesses it. This is why it must never end up in the wrong hands!

The crab and I cried out in outrage, but the wizard wasn't finished. "As for the GOLDEN PEARL, I have turned that into the Black Pearl around my neck! And now you, who have dared to CHALLENGE me, will get the end you deserve!" he continued.

The wizard turned to Chatterclaws. "You will end up in my soup!" he cried.

Then he turned to me. "And you will give me what is mine. The golden chain with the six enchanted charms. The moment for my REVENGE against Blossom has come! As soon as I have all of the charms, no one will be able to defeat me!" he declared.

The wizard held the pearl, which grew **larger**. It began to show us visions. On the surface were *terrifying* pictures of people forced into slavery, and Blossom as the wizard's prisoner!

"This will be the fate of the **KINGDOM OF FANTASY** as soon as I have the power!" he said, triumphantly.

I'd like to say I thought of something clever to say in return, but I didn't. Instead, I burst into tears. *How humiliating!*

At the wizard's command, the squid grabbed the necklace with the six charms from my neck. Then it **STRETCHED** out another tentacle and grabbed Chatterclaws.

The wizard laughed *cruelly*. "I've won, rodent! But before I begin to conquer the Kingdom of Fantasy, I will celebrate . . . with a nice bowl of **CRAB SOUP**!"

I was thrown back into the prison until . . .

a **MIRACLE** happened!

Finn appeared at my window, accompanied by a **HUGE** white whale.

The **WHALE** smacked the window with its tail, until the bars broke . . . and I was free!

Bang!

OH, WHAT A WAY TO GO!

I slipped out of the **PRISON** and saw that Finn was accompanied by all kinds of sea creatures. I met a squid with big **BULGING** eyes, who stuck out a tentacle and shook my paw. "I know what you did for my friend Finn! Thank you!"

A big scorpion fish nodded in agreement, and a young sardine swam over and gave me a high five with his tail.

I opened my eyes **wide** in astonishment. I had never encountered so many sea creatures in my life! There were tunas, lobsters, oysters, squids, **SEA URCHINS**, and more . . . and they were all SINGING!

I smiled. I never imagined I'd feel so at **HOME**

SONG OF THE SEA CREATURES

We are the creatures of the sea!
We choose our friends quite carefully.
If you are kind, honest, caring,
and good,
you are so welcome in
our neighborhood!
We care for each other,
it's our rule underwater.
We protect everyone—every son,
every daughter.
Our motto is simple:
If you help others shine,
it will make your life brighter,
and you'll feel quite divine!

under the sea! I mean, usually I prefer sitting in my beach chair to **swimming** in the ocean.

But a second later I had a terrible thought. The Wizard of the Black Pearl was about to turn Chatterclaws into **crab soup**!

Oh, what a way to go!

Quickly, I told the group of sea creatures about

THERE ARE TWO IDENTICAL FISH. CAN YOU FIND THEM?

my crab friend's situation. "The wizard has him **IMPRISONED** in his kitchen!" I cried.

A chorus of **ANGRY** protests rose from the crowd. I guess the thought of a B°iLiNg crab would get any group of sea creatures **riLeD** up.

A message began to spread throughout the sea like a beating drum: "EVERYONE COME TOGETHER

We're with you!

Answer: They're the two round, light pink fish!

TO FIGHT THE EVIL WIZARD OF THE BLACK PEARL!"

Immediately, many other sea creatures arrived. I saw sharks, orcas, and **ENORMOUSE** eels who shouted, "**Down with the wizard!**"

I must say, it was pretty impressive to see all of the creatures banding together. That day would definitely go down in **OCEAN** history as the day not a single fish ate another fish, because they were working together to fight the evil Wizard of the Black Pearl.

A dolphin swam up to me. "Climb aboard, friend!" he said. "We will **LEAD** the way to the wizard's cave!

Rats! I was hoping maybe someone else would lead the way (like a **WHALE**) and I could follow behind at a safe distance (like maybe a few miles back!).

Still, what could I do? I **jumped** aboard, and we took off.

We're off to see the wizard!

We reached the entrance to the Cave of Deepest Darkness, the place where the Wizard of the Black Pearl had established his KINGDOM.

As I got closer, I smelled a terrible odor coming from that terrifying place . . . It was the smell of nightmares!

WE'RE FREE!

The entrance to the **cave** looked like an enormouse mouth ready to devour us!

Oh, why did I have to keep **DREAMING** and ending up in these crazy adventures?! Let's face it, they were always horribly **SCARY**, filled with evil characters. It was enough to give a mouse a **nervous** breakdown!

Still, there was no time to think about it now. I had to find the crab. So I slid off the dolphin and forced myself to enter the wizard's creepy cavern.

The cavern was an **immense** palace in the shape of a huge fish **SKELETON**. It had a long central hallway with many other hallways breaking away from it.

At the end of each hallway was a prison cell, where many fish were caged.

There were prison cells for **LARGE** fish, **MEDIUM** fish, and LITTLE fish. The TINIEST fish, though, were shut up in special nets. Enormouse sea creatures, like whales, were held at the bottom of the **sea** with gigantic chains attached to their tails. Crustaceans, meanwhile, were imprisoned in nets made of **WOVEN** seaweed, and at the back of the cavern there were special nurseries for the baby fish.

I rushed from room to room, searching *anxiously* for the kitchen where I knew **Chatterclaws** had been taken.

And each time I met an imprisoned fish, I threw open the door of its cell.

"**WE'RE FREE!**" each one cried, happily.

All of the sea creatures that I freed joined our group. There were lots of **tearful** reunions. After all, some of the fish that had been CAPTURED by the wizard hadn't seen their relatives and friends in years.

"My goodness, look how **long** you've grown!" one mackerel said to another.

"I hardly recognized you with those pincers!" a starfish said to a lobster.

You're free!

I was getting a little teary-eyed watching these reunions. Now I was more determined than ever to find Chatterclaws.

At last, we turned down a **dark** corridor that led right to . . . the wizard's kitchen! And there, hanging over a pot of **BOILING** water was Chatterclaws!

With a horrified cry, I raced toward him and cut the net that held him. The crab clung to me sobbing like a baby, "I knew you'd come for me, Whatsyourname!"

I tried not to start sobbing myself. Don't get me wrong, I was **HAPPY** to see the crab, but his pincers were digging into my fur. **Ouch!**

At that moment, I heard a **RUMBLING** laugh behind me. Something told me it wasn't another happy sea creature reunion.

I turned and saw that the Wizard of the Black Pearl was standing at the kitchen door,

sneering with satisfaction. "Excellent! Tonight at dinner along with the crab soup, I will also have **SCRAMBLED MOUSE!**"

Cheese sticks! I was about to **Faint** from fear when I remembered all of the sea creatures that were there to help me.

"You don't **scare** me!" I told the wizard, taking a step toward him.

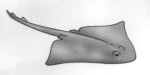

DESTROY THEM!

The wizard laughed again and snapped his fingers. Suddenly, the immense palace began to *disappear*. It had just been an illusion!

Before I could react, the wizard **snapped** his fingers again. This time, the giant squid appeared and raised up the wizard's seashell throne.

The wizard pointed to us and ordered the squid, **"DESTROY THEM!"**

The squid headed for me, but I jumped onto the back of a **WHITE** whale. Just in time!

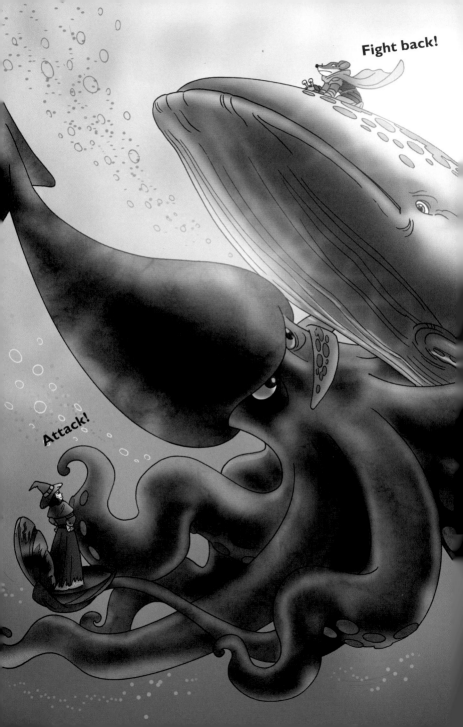

Huh?!

Ahhh!

The squid lashed out, but the whale responded with a **smack** of his strong tail. A terrifying duel began.

I held on to the back of the whale for dear life. If only I had thought to pack a **HELMET** or some goggles or maybe a gigantic shield . . .

Just when I thought things couldn't get any scarier, the wizard snapped his fingers again and transformed the whale into a **TINY PINK STARFISH!**

Suddenly, I found myself seated on nothing, and I sank head over tail. Aaaaah!

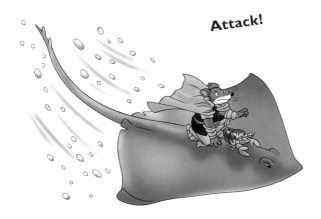

I would have HURTLED into the abyss if a stingray hadn't caught me on her soft back.

The ray smacked the squid hard with its **long** tail, **knocking** the wizard off his throne.

Then a strange thing happened. As the wizard fell, his hat flew off his head and he screamed. At first I thought he was embarrassed because he was having a bad **HAIR** day, but then I realized it was more than that.

Attack!

"My hat! I need my hat! I'm POWERLESS without my hat!" the wizard shrieked.

I couldn't believe it! So that was the wizard's secret. His hat had **MAGICAL** powers! Who would have guessed?

We watched in amazement as the wizard and his hat began tumbling into the abyss. Luckily, right before he fell I yanked the golden chain with the enchanted charms from around his neck.

YOU MEAN THIS?

After the wizard disappeared, the giant squid blinked. His eyes no longer looked cold. He smiled *warmly* at me.

"Thank you, Knight, for breaking the SPELL cast on me by the evil **Wizard of the Black Pearl**! At last I am free!"

You're free!

I smiled at him. "No problem, Sid," I said, feeling happy. But when I looked down at the golden chain with the six enchanted charms, a wave of sadness hit me. The seventh charm, the GOLDEN PEARL, had just fallen into the abyss with the wizard.

"I just wish I could have completed my mission. But the Pearl is lost forever." I sighed.

At that point, Chatterclaws SCUTTLED into his shell. When he returned, he was carrying a large dark object. "You mean this whatchamacallit?" the crab asked. He was holding up the wizard's pearl!

"Pretty good, huh?" Chatterclaws chuckled.

"B-b-but how did you get it?" I stammered, perplexed.

The crab just winked. "Let's just say, I don't have these pincer claws for nothing!" he said.

Just then, the Black Pearl gave off a strong flash

of light. A moment later it transformed back into the shimmering **GOLDEN PEARL**!

I was so excited I wanted to do a **backflip**, but since I can barely manage a forward roll I settled for a happy squeak. **OVERWHELMED**, I added the Golden Pearl to the chain with the other charms and placed the chain around my neck. I counted the charms: **ONE**, the Coral Heart; **TWO**, the Clasping Hands; **THREE**, the Medallion of the Sun and the Moon; **FOUR**, the Diamond Star; **FIVE**, the Crystal Feather; **SIX**, the Silver Unicorn; **seven**, the Golden Pearl . . .

At last, the chain was complete!

Suddenly, another blaze of light enveloped everything. In a flash, I was no longer in the

DEEP sea, but at the Crystal Castle, in Blossom's court!

"Welcome back,
Knight of the Seven Seas!
I knew that you would
complete your mission!"

The Kingdom of Fantasy has been saved!

HOORAY FOR THE KNIGHT!

"Huh? What? Who?" I babbled.

What a totally **strange** feeling. One minute, I was under the water, hanging out with lobsters and squids and all kinds of fish. And the next minute, I was inside a *beautiful* castle in the clouds!

I looked up to find Blossom, all the fairies of the court, and many other friends from the Kingdom of Fantasy staring at me.

I coughed and patted my head, pulling a piece of **seaweed** out of my ear. Oh, how embarrassing!

At that moment everyone began cheering.

"HOORAY FOR THE KNIGHT OF THE SEVEN SEAS!"

I gave the golden chain with the seven enchanted charms to Blossom, bowing so low that my whiskers **brushed** the ground.

She placed it around her neck and it seemed to SHINE a bit more brightly. Then she announced to all, "I, Queen Blossom, would like to honor this *brave* hero, who faced danger at the cost of his own life, who fought the evil Wizard of the Black Pearl, saving the entire **KINGDOM OF FANTASY**! From now on, I will be the sole guardian of the chain so that its great power will be used for peace, not for destruction."

After Blossom's speech, I saw many friends who I had met in my earlier **ADVENTURES** in the Kingdom of Fantasy.

There was *Scribblehopper*, the literary frog, who helped me fight against the **evil** witch Cackle. He wanted to be an author (but he wrote terrible poems).

I'm at your service!

"Listen to this **POEM** about Queen Blossom," he said, and began reciting, *"Oh, the queen is sweet and kind, she's like a watermelon rind . . ."*

Luckily, he was interrupted by the **CHAMELEON** Boils, who helped me on my second voyage to the Kingdom of Fantasy. One thing you should know about Boils: He loves **CHOCOLATE**!

He **tugged** on my cape just then and asked,

I am
Scribblehopper!

"Knight, you don't happen to have some chocolate, do you?"

I tried to explain that I didn't have any candy with me, but then someone else grabbed my cape. It was Goose Blahblah, also known as Goose Loose Lips, Goose Chatterbox, Goose Big Mouth, Goose . . . well, you get the idea. She LOVED to talk!

"OMG! I just knew you would find that charm!

I said, if anyone can find that **charm**, it's that knight! Yep, the knight can do it! I mean, I'm very good at **PREDICTING** these things, and —" rambled Goose Blahblah until I felt like my ears might fall off!

Right then I heard a cough, and someone **PINCHED** me on the tail. I turned around and discovered Chatterclaws.

"Excuse me, Sir Knight, but, um, I have something **IMPORTANT** to ask you," he said. "You see, I'm planning on getting whatdoyoucallit with Whatsherface, and I wanted to know if you would be my whatsit."

He pulled out a large **sparkling** diamond ring from his shell and held it up to me.

As usual, I had no idea what the crab was trying to

say. "Sorry —" I started to say.

But before I could finish, someone **pinched** my fur. I turned and saw a pretty crab with a pink shell and a wedding VEIL on her head.

Suddenly, I remembered seeing a FRAMED

photo of this same crab in the Chatterhouse. Immediately, I understood. It was Classyclaws, the crab Chatterclaws loved!

She smiled and said, "Chatterclaws asked me to **marry** him, and I've accepted. He would love it if you could be his best mouse."

Of course I accepted. What are friends for?

Chatterclaws   Classyclaws

Chatterclaws scuttled into the Chatterhouse and came out wearing an elegant black top hat.

Then Blossom led us into an immense room, **CROWDED** with gnomes and kings and dragons and elves from all of the various lands in the Kingdom of Fantasy. There was the King of the Gnomes and his wife; Sterling, the Princess of the Silver Dragons; the wise **AZUL**, the King of Sapphire City; and even Sid, the **GIANT SQUID**. In the crowd, I noticed dragons, pixies, trolls, ogres, fairies, and fish. They had all come in together in **PEACE**.

Chatterclaws stood under a large column decorated with white roses. He presented Classyclaws with the beautiful diamond ring.

"I **LOVE** you more than any other whoosy whatsit in the world!" he proclaimed.

"I **LOVE** you, too!" Classyclaws replied, taking the ring with a grin.

Blossom took the hand of her husband, George, the king of the Kingdom of Dreams, and announced, "By the laws of the Kingdom of Fantasy, we declare you **HUSBAND AND WiFE!**"

At that point everyone clapped and cheered, **"Hooray for the happy couple!"**

Then Chatterclaws shouted, "And now who's ready to PARTY like a crab?!"

The crowd **ERUPTED** in more cheers as everyone headed off to the reception area.

I wasn't sure what to expect. I mean, I've never been to a crab wedding before! But it really was a **MAGICAL** sight.

There were tables with food (too bad it was seaweed!) and there was a **pool** for the aquatic guests.

But when I spotted Finn and went over to say hello, I slipped and fell into the water, sinking **down, down, down** . . .

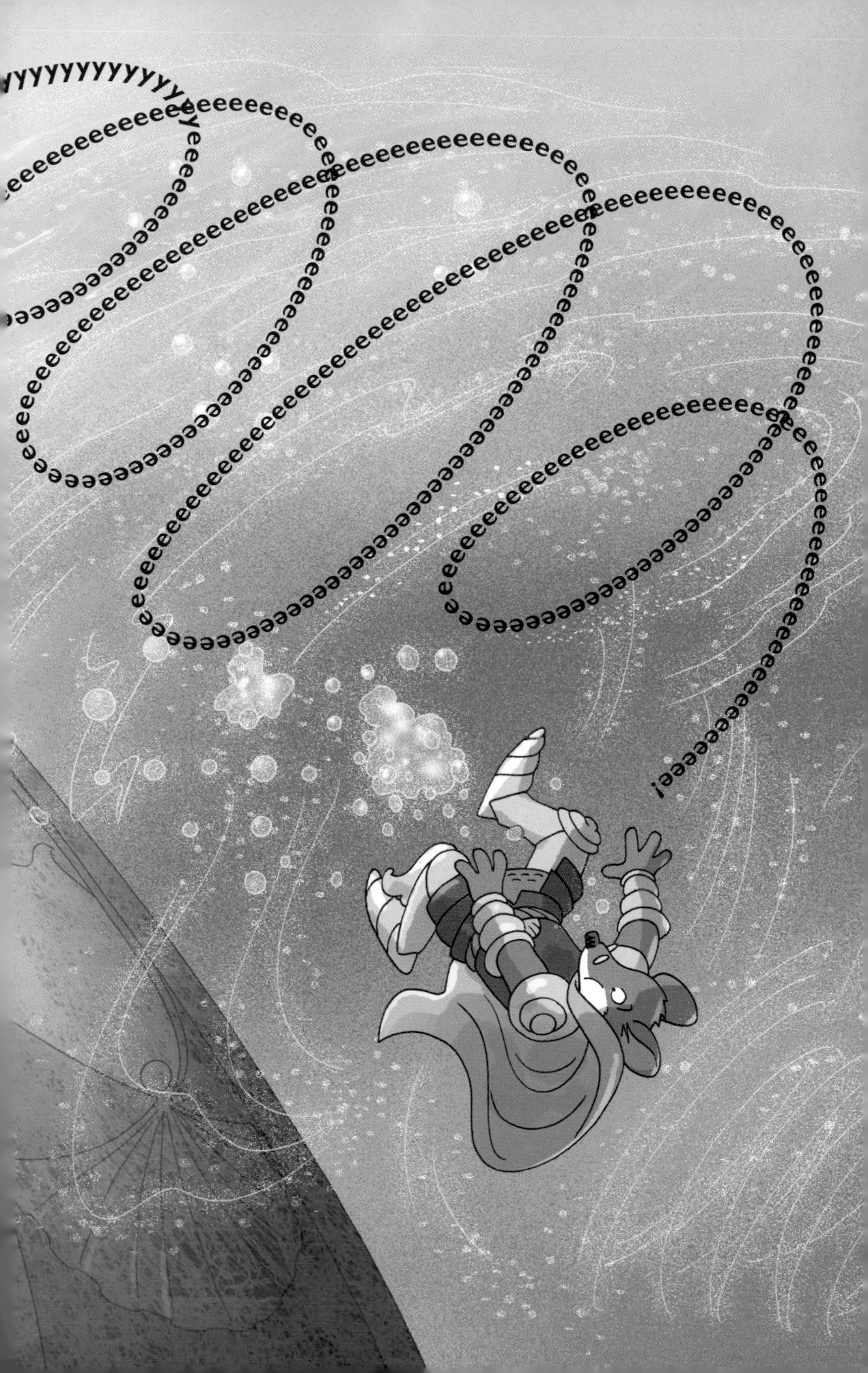

ARE YOU
AWAKE?

Just then someone shook me gently by the paw, and I heard a familiar voice saying, **"Are you awake?"**

Huh? What was going on? Where was Finn? What happened to the crab wedding?

I opened my **EYES** and saw my nephew Benjamin bending over me!

What was Benjamin doing in the **KINGDOM OF FANTASY?**

Or maybe . . .

If Benjamin was in front of me . . .

. . . then I was no longer in the Kingdom of Fantasy!

"Where am I?" I mumbled.

"Uncle, you're on **Pink Seashell**

Beach!" Benjamin squeaked. "Don't you remember?"

Of course, it was all coming back to me. I was on the beach in **NEW MOUSE CITY**. Yes, this is where my *FABUMOUSE* adventure had started!

The **ORANGE SODA** in my glass was now hot. The sand beneath my paws was no longer **burning**. And the shadows had grown **long**, because the sun was setting . . .

To me, it had seemed like a **long journey**, but I guess it had lasted only one afternoon!

For a moment, I looked around for my friend Chatterclaws. "Did you happen to see a **CRAB** wearing a top hat go by?" I asked Benjamin.

My nephew looked at me. "I think you've been out in the SUN too long, Uncle," he said with a worried expression.

Then I remembered. It was all just a DREAM, just like all the other times I had visited the Kingdom of Fantasy.

"I'm okay, Benjamin," I said. And I was.

I had slept, I had dreamed, and now I would be able to write my book.

And I must say, this story would be pretty

amazing. How many times have you read about a **TUNa TaXI**, or a cow with butterfly wings, or a fancy crab wedding?

Of course, thinking about the crab wedding got me thinking about Chatterclaws. I would miss my new friend. A **WAVE** of sadness hit me.

"Let's get going," I said to Benjamin.

But then, as were packing up, I saw something out by the rocks. I stood up. It was a familiar-looking shell, TEETERING on a rock. The **shell** was moving very slowly.

Was it . . . ? Could it be . . . ?

I know it sounds crazy. After all, my friends from the Kingdom of Fantasy only exist in my dreams. But I **jumped** up and ran toward the shell anyway.

But when I reached the rock, the shell had already tumbled gently into the sea.

Ah, well. I may never end up knowing the

TRUTH about that shell. Part of me would like to think it really was Chatterclaws waving good-bye to me. Maybe I can ask him the next time I visit the **KINGDOM OF FANTASY**!

I Did It!

I took Benjamin home. Then I ran to my office. Even thought it was **late**, everyone was still there waiting for me. I ran inside and announced, "**I did it! I had a dream!**"

Their faces all **LIT** up.

"Now you can write another Kingdom of Fantasy book!" my assistant, Mousella, cried excitedly.

I decided I would be more productive if I wrote my book from home, so my coworkers walked me there. Then my grandfather **locked** me into my home office and threw the **key** into the thick bushes outside my house. "I'm doing it for your own good, Grandson," he squeaked. "Only come out when you're done *writing*!"

For once, I wasn't worried. I rushed to my computer and began to write:

"It was a stunning summer night in New Mouse City..."

I wrote and wrote and wrote without stopping. Well, okay, I did stop to nibble on a chocolate Cheesy Chew or two (or three) . . .

Snooore!

I continued to write for **DAYS** and **DAYS** and **DAYS**, until I had a long beard and **gray** fur and walked with a cane. All right, it didn't take exactly *that* long, but it did seem like I was writing *forever*. The Kingdom of Fantasy is such an incredible place, I wanted to make sure I remembered every little thing about my adventure!

Finally, I finished *writing* and shut off my computer. Then I fell asleep for a few hours and woke up **drooling** on my keyboard (don't tell my grandfather!).

And now my seventh adventure in the Kingdom of Fantasy has been published! It's called The Enchanted Charms.

Yes, it is the book you are reading right now.

Did you like it? I hope so!

It is dedicated to you, my dear readers, because I know you are just as **FANTASTIC** as the **KINGDOM OF FANTASY**!

I love you all!

Your mouse friend,

Geronimo Stilton

You are fantastic!

FANTASIAN ALPHABET

ABOUT THE AUTHOR

Born in New Mouse City, Mouse Island, **GERONIMO STILTON** is Rattus Emeritus of Mousomorphic Literature and of Neo-Ratonic Comparative Philosophy. For the past twenty years, he has been running *The Rodent's Gazette*, New Mouse City's most widely read daily newspaper.

Stilton was awarded the Ratitzer Prize for his scoops on *The Curse of the Cheese Pyramid* and *The Search for Sunken Treasure*. He has also received the Andersen 2000 Prize for Personality of the Year. One of his bestsellers won the 2002 eBook Award for world's best ratlings' electronic book. His works have been published all over the globe.

In his spare time, Mr. Stilton collects antique cheese rinds and plays golf. But what he most enjoys is telling stories to his nephew Benjamin.

Be sure to read all my adventures in the Kingdom of Fantasy!

THE KINGDOM OF FANTASY

THE QUEST FOR PARADISE:
THE RETURN TO THE KINGDOM OF FANTASY

THE AMAZING VOYAGE:
THE THIRD ADVENTURE IN THE KINGDOM OF FANTASY

THE DRAGON PROPHECY:
THE FOURTH ADVENTUR IN THE KINGDOM OF FANTASY

THE VOLCANO OF FIRE:
THE FIFTH ADVENTURE IN THE KINGDOM OF FANTASY

THE SEARCH FOR TREASURE:
THE SIXTH ADVENTURE IN THE KINGDOM OF FANTASY

THE ENCHANTED CHARMS:
THE SEVENTH ADVENTURE IN THE KINGDOM OF FANTASY

Don't miss any of my other fabumouse adventures!

#1 Lost Treasure of the Emerald Eye

#2 The Curse of the Cheese Pyramid

#3 Cat and Mouse in a Haunted House

#4 I'm Too Fond of My Fur!

#5 Four Mice Deep in the Jungle

#6 Paws Off, Cheddarface!

#7 Red Pizzas for a Blue Count

#8 Attack of the Bandit Cats

#9 A Fabumouse Vacation for Geronimo

#10 All Because of a Cup of Coffee

#11 It's Halloween, You 'Fraidy Mouse!

#12 Merry Christmas, Geronimo!

#13 The Phantom of the Subway

#14 The Temple of the Ruby of Fire

#15 The Mona Mousa Code

#16 A Cheese-Colored Camper

#17 Watch Your Whiskers, Stilton!

#18 Shipwreck on the Pirate Islands

#19 My Name Is Stilton, Geronimo Stilton

#20 Surf's Up, Geronimo!

#21 The Wild, Wild West

#22 The Secret of Cacklefur Castle

A Christmas Tale

#23 Valentine's Day Disaster

#24 Field Trip to Niagara Falls

#25 The Search for Sunken Treasure

#26 The Mummy with No Name

#27 The Christmas Toy Factory

#28 Wedding Crasher

#29 Down and Out Down Under

#30 The Mouse Island Marathon

#31 The Mysterious Cheese Thief

Christmas Catastrophe

#32 Valley of the Giant Skeletons

#33 Geronimo and the Gold Medal Mystery

#34 Geronimo Stilton, Secret Agent

#35 A Very Merry Christmas

#36 Geronimo's Valentine

#37 The Race Across America

#38 A Fabumouse School Adventure

#39 Singing Sensation

#40 The Karate Mouse

#41 Mighty Mount Kilimanjaro

#42 The Peculiar Pumpkin Thief

#43 I'm Not a Supermouse!

#44 The Giant
Diamond Robbery

#45 Save the White
Whale!

#46 The Haunted
Castle

#47 Run for the Hills,
Geronimo!

#48 The Mystery in
Venice

#49 The Way of
the Samurai

#50 This Hotel Is
Haunted!

#51 The Enormouse
Pearl Heist

#52 Mouse in Space!

#53 Rumble in
the Jungle

#54 Get into Gear,
Stilton!

#55 The Golden
Statue Plot

#56 Flight of the
Red Bandit

The Hunt for the
Golden Book

#57 The Stinky
Cheese Vacation

#58 The Super
Chef Contest

#59 Welcome to
Moldy Manor

The Hunt for the
Curious Cheese

#60 The Treasure of
Easter Island

Check out these very special editions!

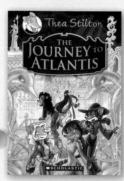

THEA STILTON: THE JOURNEY TO ATLANTIS

THEA STILTON: THE SECRET OF THE FAIRIES

THEA STILTON: THE SECRET OF THE SNOW

THE JOURNEY THROUGH TIME

BACK IN TIME: THE SECOND JOURNEY THROUGH TIME